Hamiltonians

HAMILTONIANS

Peter Abbot

Rock's Mills Press
Oakville, Ontario
2018

Published by
ROCK'S MILLS PRESS
www.rocksmillspress.com

An earlier version of this novel was published in a limited edition under the title *Hear the Children* in 2017 by Rock's Mills Press.

Cover illustration: Panoramio Rokker/Wikimedia

For information, please contact the publisher:
customer.service@rocksmillspress.com

ISBN-13: 978-1-77244-126-0
ISBN-13: 978-1-77244-127-7 (Amazon edition)
ISBN-13: 978-1-77244-128-4 (Kindle ebook)

Contents

MILLENNIAL MURDERS

We are stunned. The new century has brought suffering and death to our city.

Two citizens of Hamilton have been brutally murdered. In what may have been a tragic coincidence, it would appear that both victims lost their lives on the same night, Saturday 13 January. Nearly a week later, the murderer or murderers have not been apprehended.

In West Hamilton, a young boy and his mother were viciously attacked; the mother has survived, but her young son, who at first seemed less severely injured, died yesterday in hospital, after four days in intensive care. The mother's 29-year-old husband, who is not the boy's natural father, is being sought for questioning. He had been released from Maplehurst Detention Centre a few days earlier, and had previously served prison sentences for various offences relating to drugs and alcohol, including an earlier assault on his wife.

Only hours earlier, apparently, a young man was murdered in a luxurious penthouse apartment in downtown Hamilton, in what a police spokesperson described as a gangland-style slaying. He too had a criminal record and had been released only recently from prison. His body was not discovered for three days.

It is speculated that the two slayings may be connected, and that both may also be connected with the mysterious disappearance of an Ancaster resident who also has a criminal record and is being sought in the United States and throughout South America, where it is suspected he has fled.

These facts have been reported widely in the media, as many of you will know.

1

What do they have to do with any of our readers? Of course all Hamiltonians must be alarmed that at least one violent and probably desperate criminal is still at large. The police advise vigilance, and extreme caution when approaching strangers.

We must also hope that, despite well-publicized financial cutbacks, our police forces are putting forward all necessary efforts and resources toward solving the two cases in the quickest possible time, apprehending the man or men responsible for such heinous crimes. Our community cannot tolerate vicious, destructive behaviors.

However, must we not, all of us, try to understand why these horrific events have afflicted our city at this time, and work to prevent any recurrence? Do we bear, each of us, any responsibility, however limited?

As many of you will know, one commentator has claimed that Hamilton is now destined to become notorious as "Canada's Murder Capital"! We do not agree. Nor do we agree that "the notorious decay of Hamilton's core" has anything to do with random acts of destruction. Two murders, even such horrific murders as these that have marred the beginning of our Millennium, do not define our society or, indeed, establish a trend.

Hamilton is a peaceful community. Its criminal past is just that - past. However, we must all be vigilant. We must question ourselves constantly. Do we condone violence in our everyday lives? Do we work to reduce violence wherever and whenever it occurs? Do we protect our children as well as we should?

A reputation, once lost, is not easily regained. Hamilton's well-earned reputation as a progressive, positive, peaceful and ambitious society must be valued and protected by us all.

We owe that to our families, our friends, our neighbours, our entire community.

—NEWSPAPER EDITORIAL

ONE
A Ticket for Tina

I won't say a whole lot about my relationship with Marv. Too complicated. And irrelevant here - or anywhere. Let's just say we were buddies in the old days, then I married and fell out of that messy wasteful self-defeating lifestyle, and he was one of the guys I lost touch with. A good thing too. I worked hard after that, got to know some seriously mobile older men, spoke to them respectfully, "Sir", got myself a job, settled into being a good hockey dad as my two kids grew into good Canadian boys.

So I didn't know who it was when Marv called me one afternoon. One of those long-distance-sounding collect calls that always trouble me with memories of my mother when she was dying of cancer - my sister in the US of A would call me that way for news, "I'm so worried, Bri, wish I could be there, but you know -", she was short of money, living with an alcoholic.

"This Is Bell Canada. You have a Collect Call from"

"Old Buddy."

Old Buddy?

"You may Press One Now to Accept the Charges, Press Two to Refuse the Charges, Or Answer One of the Following Questions -"

I pressed One.

"Hi there." Faintly familiar voice, I couldn't place it.

"Hey, who's that?"

"Marv, you remember Marv, Old Buddy? 'Course you do."

Of course I did. Marv. "So where are you, Marv?"

"In jail."

"In - Did you say jail?"

"Yeah. Long story, Old Buddy. Tell it to you one day, when I get out? No justice for the wicked. So you're straight and narrow?"

"You could say that."

"And rich? You were always one to hold onto the pennies - lots of cents, ha ha?"

"No, you couldn't say that, Marv. Got a wife and two kids. But I make out all right. So?"

"Would you do something for me, Old Buddy? Easy, won't cost you. Favour for a friend of mine, that's all. Favour for me."

I should have remembered then what I remembered later. About Marv. That he was always full of bullshit, you never knew exactly where you were with him. Why he was so popular, I guess - always bellowing some great joke you had heard before, some wild story you couldn't believe, non-stop entertainment. But the guys who knew him better than I ever did would keep some distance between Marv and themselves. You got to notice this - and how you bought him more beers than he ever bought you. Hey, that's life. I had a ball too, in those days. Sort of. I was remembering some of that while we spoke. Nostalgia? Nostalgia.

"So what is it? You all right, Marv?" But I tried to make my voice flat, cool. Didn't want to sound eager to fork out money, or get involved with his life in any way.

"Well, it's this guy I know in here? He's a great guy. I'd do it if I was out, get him what he wants - and he'll be out in a couple weeks - but that'll be too late for him to buy any tickets, they're going real fast - it's her last tour - Tina Turner's, you remember how we used to, how all the guys used to - what a voice, what a doll, hey? The one and only Tina Turner! - we all thought she was great, hey? What a woman! Well, Tiger wants to be there. Says he *got* to be there. The show in Toronto? Her last performance in Canada, she's retiring from show biz? It's real important for him to be there. So, I thought of you - you been in entertainment -"

"Entertainment, Marv? What do you mean, entertainment?"

"You were in all those plays. In high school, remember? And you always sang along with Tina Turner and all those others - Gordon Lightfoot, Anne Murray, all those, when we - you remember, the nickelodeon, is that what it was called? In the sports bar? 'Course now they got karaoke. And you had that great voice. Always loved to hear you sing, Old Buddy! You had this really great voice. And you wrote poetry, and that story in the school magazine -"

Yes, I was always good at singing along. Not singing, I mean - singing *along*. Then. Especially when I was juiced up. No, I don't sing any more, now, Marv - not even in the shower. Do I miss that? No. Yes - well, yes, just sometimes. Like maybe now - now you remind me.

"So Marv - you want me to buy a ticket for your friend? Is that it?" Abrupt - let's end this.

"Four tickets, Old Buddy. For him and his three friends. You wouldn't mind, would you? Just go to the nearest Ticketmaster, but you got to do it quick, they're going real fast. That would be great, real great. That would be a real favour. And I'll pay you back, Old Buddy, I promise. When I'm out - soon as I'm out? I'll call you and we'll meet in the old place, hey, for old times' sake, and we'll catch up, talk about the old times, hey - we'll get to know each other again, hey, I'd like that."

"And how would I get the tickets to your friend? Send them to *you*?"

"No. I'll give you his mother's address. You just put them in an envelope and send them to her? He'll get them soon as he's out. She's in Toronto." Muffled, turning to the friend for the address. Which he then read out to me. I wrote it down.

"Right. I'll do that, Marv. Hey, you look after yourself."

"Yeah, I will. And you too. I'm - hey, I'm grateful, I'm real grateful, Old Buddy? You always were a great friend, know that? A real friend."

Pause. And my name's not Old Buddy, Marv: my name's Brian. I almost said that. Resentfully. Why resentfully? And why do I feel a sort of guilt as I hold the phone and breathe into it and hear his rough breathing at the other end?

At last - "Right, Marv. I'll do that soon as I can. Today. And I'll send the tickets to your friend's mother. So. I hope he'll enjoy it. Tina Turner's final tour, hey?"

"Yeah. Who would of thought it? He says she looks just as sexy and she sings just as good. The one and only! Remember when we used to - "

But I didn't want this. I didn't want Marv to remind me any more about the past, about my wasted wasteful youth, about the bad time - and the good times. I didn't want him to reconnect me with that life, with himself. I didn't want him in my mind, my memory, my life.

"I got to go, Marv. It's busy in here - I - You look after yourself. Good talking to you. Look after yourself. Bye now."

Well, to cut a long story short - before you get even more bored than you are, whoever you are, reading this. Who am I writing this for, anyway? Why? - So I asked Marianne to get the tickets, which she did, that afternoon - apparently there was a Ticketmaster in Copps Coliseum and she wanted to go there anyways to get tickets for a hockey game for her son, so it worked out good. I gave her a blank check with appropriate identification (never let your Visa out of your sight!), and told her to get the cheapest set of four she could, and I was surprised and annoyed to find that it cost over $500! Well, I guess that didn't quite break the bank, but I didn't expect the tickets to cost that much. Marianne said the show was almost sold out, she could have gotten a cheaper single ticket, but not four together - so - Well, there it was. I sent them off addressed to Marv's friend's mother.

And it *was* a busy period, getting on for Christmas, Festive Season, all that, and we wanted to move more vehicles - needed to. So I didn't think any more about Marv and the whole Tina Turner thing, until, a couple days ago, I happened to hear a passing comment about the show on my car radio, what a great great *great* show it had been!

And that morning, another sudden unexpected connection with my past. A guy comes in to look at one of the new models, and he looks at me after a moment and says "Brian! Hey, it's years. Brian. It's Brett, remember me? I didn't have a moustache then, and I weighed a few kilos less, eh? But you look about the same, Buddy, how do you do it? I bet you work out twice a day in some fancy expensive gym with a lot of sexy females gyrating round you! The good life, eh? Nice work if you can get it!"

And as I was fending him off with chat, I don't know why but I mentioned Marv's name, and then the Tina Turner show, and before I could explain the connection and was beginning to regret what I'd already said, and I'd have to say he called me from jail, Brett interrupted. "Marv - surely you know all about Marv? Would you ever have suspected? Old Marv, old bullshitting Marv, always those big stories, all the women he knew, maybe we should have wondered why he was always telling us all that bullshit. It gave *me* a shock, I can tell you."

"What? What did?"

"Oh, you *don't* know. Maybe you wouldn't have spoken to him if you *had* known - I know *I* wouldn't ever speak to him again if I happened to bump into him, which thank God I won't. He's a *pedophile*, Brian! Didn't you know? Child molester, sexual abuse of little kids - a fuckin pedophile. They found him with some missing kids he was with. Couple years ago. Got a long sentence, if I remember right. But not long enough. So he called you from jail? He should be Inside for half his life. Should be in for *all* his life, right? You got kids? I got three. We got to protect them, eh, *all* our kids, from guys like that - we got to put all pedophiles away. This society's too soft on guys like that!

They *seem* good guys, that's how they attract kids, they seem harmless, but they're twisted deep down. They rape kids, they kill kids. And you know it's been proved they can never change, they just do it over and over if you let them. So we got to lock them away, right? Would be better to get rid of them, *really* get rid of them, not let them lie around and eat good meals and watch TV and have a good time, all at our expense, our taxes, but Canadians are too soft to do the right thing, eh. We even let them out, back into society so they can do it again, kill more kids. Bleeding hearts, we're bleeding hearts, right? Canadians are bleeding bloody hearts. But we got to put them where they can't get at our kids."

Quite some speech, that, Brett!

Next day I found I was thinking again about Marv, and Tina Turner. Wondering what was really going on there. I told the story to a guy I knew who was a lawyer, and he said "Oh you know, don't you, what he was up to? Your Marv? That's one way they can get money in prison, to buy drugs etcetera, and also he maybe needed a protector - being a pedophile, he's got lots of enemies, death-threats. They get a friend or relative to put money into another inmate's account, outside, and then he provides a proportion to your guy inside - probably the other one's boss man in the range, he controls the canteen - or in your Marv's case he was getting you to provide a big expensive favour for his so-called friend, who would return the favour - money or more likely protection, or influence, whatever. He may not've sounded - they get to be good actors in there, you know - but he may have been desperate, your Marv - you say he wasn't ever a close friend of yours, just an acquaintance you hadn't seen for a good long while, so why does he call *you*? Now? Out of the blue? It's a whole different society in there, Brian, a whole different life. You wouldn't want to know. You really wouldn't want to know."

So. But I still think about Marv. I don't want to - but I do. But what could I do to help him? Does he even *deserve* help? If he *can* be helped, really helped? He may even be dead, now, for all I know, stabbed to death while exercising, like in that movie, I can't remember what it was called. And - why bother? What can I do about any of it, assuming he's alive? Nothing, nothing. And, hey, he owes *me* - $500! - I don't owe *him*. Why am I even thinking about him? He wasn't even a close friend, just a school and hockey and boozing pal. A good long while ago. But a *pedophile*! Marv! How could he be a pedophile - someone like that, just a regular guy, popular, friendly, just a normal friendly guy?

I also found myself thinking about the Tina Turner show, and Marv's friend and the others sitting there watching her, listening to her.

The One and Only! Strutting her stuff! I hope they enjoyed the show.

And why have I been lying like this? Well, I didn't exactly lie to Marv - just concealed the truth. Which is that I'm a lawyer, not a car salesman, though I did earn a few dollars, years ago, helping in my uncle's business, in the summer, as a school-kid - But maybe he *did* know - that I'm a lawyer - and maybe that's why he called me, after so many years? Could be. Guess I was mainly on my guard with Marv just because he's in jail and I could sense trouble if - Well, there was that case not long ago of a lawyer - I didn't *know* him but I'd met him - and he was persuaded to smuggle drugs into the jail - they don't search lawyers usually, but somehow, that time - I guess they knew something, or suspected - And so - I seem to have written a short story for my sins! - or Marv's sins. Is that what it is? And now I'm remembering a whole lot more about him, how he was in the old days - a cheerful guy, always fun to be around. That was Marv.

TWO
The Hockey-Stick

No, I wasn't frightened of him. I wasn't frightened at all. He was kind. He gave me a hockey-stick and stuff. I liked him.

Yes, he was my Mum's friend. Like, boyfriend, I guess. He came home with my Mum one day and he made supper for us, it was sausage and egg and fries and stuff, we liked it. Sam liked it - Samantha - my little sister - not just me, she liked it too. It was great, it was the best supper. Then he goes Would we like it if he would take us to a movie, it was *Pokemon*, he paid for us all, it was great. He took us in his car. My Mum came too, they held hands. It was for kids, the movie was for kids, but my Mum said she liked it too.

Yes, he came to our place most nights after that night. He cooked supper and watched TV and stuff.

Into my room? Sometimes he came into my room. He would look at my comics with me, he had a lot of comics when he was my age, *Superman* and *Spiderman* specially, he collected them, he wished his Mum *didn't* thrown them all out, they would of been valuable now, he said, like a hundred dollars maybe, each one. A hundred dollars, each one! He really liked looking at my comics with me and he brung me comics too, new ones from a bookstore, and then he would read them to me and I would read them to him too, we would sit together on my bed, just the two of us, we would read to each other, he would help me with words, and it was great. Just the two of us. It was great.

What else? Together? Well, like - He came to meet us after school, Sam and me, he walked home with us, and sometimes he would take

9

us into Tim Horton's on the way, For a special treat, he goes, if we been behaving good, nice to the teacher and done good work, and if I was nice to Sam, and we had, like, ice cream or cookies and stuff, and pop. He goes Good manners, good life.

No, I didn't tell Mum about that. Going to Tim Horton's for special treats with him. Like, he goes No, not to, it's a special treat just for us three. And he goes your Mum might be sad if you tell her, cause she don't have enough money to give us special treats, cause she's a single Mum, and we shouldn't make her sad, we should try to make her happy. So I didn't tell her. But I think Sam did. And, he says he was, like, an uncle for us. Our special uncle. Not a father. I never had no father, like other kids, my Mum told me that, but I think - you have to have a father, I think every kid does have a father, like, at the beginning, but my father, he went away before I even seen him, my Gramma told me that once, before she got sick and went away. But Sam had a father. But he used to beat us, and he beat my Mum, and he would be sick in the bathroom, and then he went away and stopped sending money, and my Mum had to go to work.

No, he didn't tell us not to tell her about other things we did together. He goes It's bad to do secret things. He goes Mum is the most important person in your life and you guys must always love her best even if she's poor and can't give us things that other kids have, bikes and TV games and videos and stuff. And he gave Sam a doll that talked and stuff. And he took me to a hockey game for my birthday, we went to Toronto in his car, we saw the Maple Leafs, it was great. They won. It was great! But it was cold too, not like watching it on TV, my feet got achy, and all the people were screaming and shouting and jumping and stuff. It was great. And he gave me a special hockey-stick - Him and me, we went to Eaton's and I got to look at them all and he goes Choose whichever one you want, so I did. It was awesome.

Yes. He did touch me. He held my hand at the game sometimes. And he kissed me in the car. I go Thank you for the hockey-stick, thank you for taking me to the game, it was great, and that was when he kissed me.

No, he didn't say I mustn't tell my Mum.

Yes, I didn't tell her.

I don't know, I just didn't.

It was funny. It felt funny. Only my Mum kisses me sometimes. It felt funny when he did it. His face has whiskers and stuff. But I never had an uncle before.

No, I didn't mind. I didn't mind at all. He didn't hurt me. He was smiling. He goes You make me feel so happy, and how he liked it when it was just the two of us together. And he goes Am I happy? And how he loves me very much, and how I remind him of how he was when he was a boy. He goes I was happy too, then, when I was a little boy, a long time ago, I was happy then. And his uncle gave him a hockey-stick, just like me and him.

No, nothing else. Then we went home. I was sleepy, it was late. It was warm in the car and there was music on the radio, I went to sleep. He woke me up when we got back to Hamilton.

No, nothing else. He just carried me into our house, and put me to bed, and kissed me goodnight, and then he went.

Yes, he did kiss me, I remember that.

I don't know if she was there. My Mum goes out at night sometimes. She leaves me to look after Sam when she goes out. I was so sleepy.

Yes, he just went away after he kissed me goodnight.

No, he didn't undress me. I just lay down in my clothes, Mum says I shouldn't do that, it creases them and stuff, but sometimes if I'm sleepy I do, I just lay down and pull the blankets over me. So I did that, and then he kissed me goodnight, and turned off the light.

Yes, my Mum was there in the morning.

No, she didn't say nothing. I showed her the hockey-stick and she goes You are a very lucky boy, it must be expensive, and to be careful with it, and keep it away from Sam, so she won't get hurt, and did I say thank you, and I go Yes, I did. She didn't ask about the game, who won, it was the Maple Leafs, she was yawning and yawning. Then Sam and I went to school.

The trailer? It was for Sam's birthday. He says to my Mum he would like to give both of us kids a special treat, not just Sam, he wanted me to be with Sam 'case she would get lonely. He says Mum deserves a break, and visit her friend in Guelph, she should go, and he goes You're look-ing exhausted, you really need a break, it would be, like, a break, a little holiday for you. He says his friend has a trailer in a trailer-park, and there was a lake for swimming but it was too cold to do that, but there was slides and roundabouts and places to play and stuff, and Sam and me we could have a good time on Sam's birthday and over the weekend and till Mum comes back from Guelph. And so she goes Well - and then she goes Maybe - and then she goesYes, and we must behave the bestest we can and be extra good and do everything what he tells us.

By bus. We went there on the bus. To near the trailer-park. It was his friend's trailer.

Yes, we did have a good time. It was cold outside but it was hot in the trailer. The trailer was great, it was, like, a little house, sort of, with everything, like, close together. It had a red roof. And a little ladder. Sam slept on the top bunk and I was underneath. We played ball outside, and games and cards and stuff inside when it got dark. It was fun. And he goes It's like when I was a little boy, when I was Sam's age. When he was Sam's age, he goes, I was so happy. And it was her birthday and so we had a cake, it was a chocolate cake, it had seven candles and he lit them with matches but Sam only blew out three, so then I blew out all the others, and we sang "Happy Birthday, dear Sam" and then we played games and went to bed. It was great. It was great.

And then the policemen came.

Yes, it was at night. The second night. Sam and me, we're in bed. She was asleep, I think she was asleep, she was in the top bunk place - the top bunk? He was telling us another story. It was about a boy who ran away, his father was cruel, he beat him and beat him, and he didn't have no mother, and he ran into the forest, and there was this magic-man who talked to the birds and the animals and he said the boy could live with him in his little house in the forest. Then they banged on the door. Loud banging and when he opened it, they came in and they pushed him and they shouted at him to put his hands above his head and they had guns. They pushed him against the - against the counter? - and pulled his arms down and, like, they put things on his hands.

Handcuffs. Yes, handcuffs. And he was crying and saying he done nothing wrong and don't frighten the children and look, Sam and me were all right, look, he didn't hurt us at all, and now Sam was crying and I was crying, and he goes Ask the children, ask the children, ask the children -

No, he never hurt us, we were crying 'cause we were frightened. The policemen made us frightened, Sam was frightened, we were both crying and he was crying and she still wakes up Mum and me in the night and says the policemen are coming for her.

Yes, then they took him away and then they say to dress and then Sam and me went in another police car, with a lady policeman, she was nice, and the light on top going round and round, like, flashing in the dark, we sat in the back, and she drived us home, and Mum was there, and she was crying and she hugged us.

No, Mum didn't tell me what to say. She never did. She says not to tell any lies, just to tell the truth and all what happened, answer all the questions and, like, just tell the truth. And I never saw him after till today.

No, he never hurt me. He never would of hurt me.

THREE
Burning Bright

Hi, it's me.

Yeah, yeah, I know. You busy! But I won't be long.

Yeah, and nothing about - Yeah, 'course - I know.

But when you coming? I got things to tell you.

About this guy yesterday. Yeah, I'll be quick.

So, I gave him my usual spiel. Know it off by heart now. "I'm Brad. Five feet ten inches, with a great body. Twenty-two years old. Eight inches, cut. Thirty dollars." See, I believe in being straight - so to say. Tell them exactly what's on offer, how much, no misunderstandings, customer goes away happy. Right?

Brad? "Why Brad?" Why not? Brad Pitt - you don't like him? So it's a good name for a guy - sorta hunky-sounding? Good-looking. Stacked. Buff. No, not "pretty-boy"! Handsome, good-looking! Hey, and you can trust this guy! This Brad. Right? So it's a good name for what you - Yeah, but I wasn't going to -

Yeah, well don't get mad at me. Don't get excited, eh. And it's better than what they called me Inside, hey. You remember. Tiger! That name would scare guys off when they don't know me. Maybe attract some guys - some, maybe - but scare some too. Anyways, you should be pleased with me. I made a good start here. Like you said. And it's not a bad place - seems dead, scene's dead? But I don't really know it yet. When I was Inside here, some of the guys were from Hamilton, they told me things about the life here, but I haven't been around yet myself. I was born here, told you that, didn't I? But my Ma moved to T.O. after my dad was killed. I was just a small kid, I don't remember it hardly at all. Those years in T.O. when I was growing up, I thought Hamilton was, like, the end of the world, just a polluted burg you pass on the way to Niagara? But now I'm here, back here - well, give it a chance is what I say - see what it's got to offer, eh? Like you said. Take it easy.

Yeah, don't worry. Don't worry at all - I'm being very quiet, very careful, like you said. But what you want me to *do?* When will you - ?

'Course not! Hey, I promised, didn't I? And who I gonna talk to here, anyways? Nobody! I got *nobody* to talk to.

Yeah, yeah - no hard drugs. Learnt my lesson, yeah, you're right. I learnt my lesson. Anyways, I don't even know the scene here yet. And I got no money for drugs, you know that! I know I got to do only what I promised you, eh, and I will, don't worry. Gave you my word, hey?

Smoking-up? Hey, that's different. What you mean, you can tell? So how can you tell? I'm just in a good mood, that's all. Happy. Happy talking to you. Having a good time, all on my own. Chilling out. You should be pleased. You said to take it easy, be cool, be happy. Don't you want me to tell you everything? A bit of weed never hurt nobody, eh. You know that. *You* used to smoke-up Inside, we all did, hey? When I met you. You was the one who got me into them hard drugs, remember! I was just a pussycat before.

Now don't get mad, just joking! Well, I like joking, eh? And I got nobody to talk to here. Gets lonely at night. You want to run over and chill out with me? Too busy? See, like I say, I got *nobody.*

Don't *worry!* Hey, don't *worry!* Everything's cool. Real cool. But what you want me to *do?*

'Course I'm doing what you said. *Exactly* what you said. That advertisement was real cool.

What you mean, "ostentatious"? What's "ostentatious"?

No. It was *not* ostentatious. It was like the other ones in there - nothing special.

Yeah, under "Adult Massage", that's where it is, if you wanna look. And it just said "Brad for Pleasure, Men Only, In-calls Only, $30" and a call number, *this* call number.

Yeah, $30 is the going rate - a bit cheaper than, actually - I checked last week's before I put mine in. Some of them charge more. All the "Escorts" do.

No, no contact with any of the other guys. Like you said.

Not yet. No, that's what I thought. Four of them, adverts like I said - and I'll tell you if anyone does, if any of them, like, contact me. You don't think there's any gangs running those other ones, do you? Mafia? Hell's Angels? This is still a Mafia town, hey? That's what I heard in T.O.. Is that why you keep on saying Be careful, be careful? Anyway, I *been* careful. So don't *worry*.

Five. Altogether five calls. Two wanted to come straight away, this week. Two others were just enquiring, thinking about it, shopping around I guess, said they'll call again. Yeah, all right, I know, but -

Yeah, so it's going real good. So far. So could you put some more money in that account? Just a couple hundred?

Yeah, well I need to eat, eh, and some new clothes? To look good. You want me to look good, don't you? I want to look good for you! *When* you coming over? Hey, I'd really like to see you! You know that.

"Extravagant"? No, I won't be extravagant. "Vain"? Me vain! Hey, don't you like me now? See, I can't help being such a great good-lookin guy!

Yeah, well it's good to hear you laugh. Like when I first knew you, Inside. But now you worry, worry, *worry*. Why?

I know it. I'm grateful, you know I'm grateful. I won't mess up. See, I know it's a new beginning for me and you have great ideas for me, a great future, and I *will* be careful. I promise. How can I make you believe me? You know I always told you the truth, Inside - always. And I'm telling you the truth now. I don't want to be Inside again, never again. Don't want a shiv in my back. Wanna live my own life. And I wouldn't be here now if it wasn't for you. I know it. I'm grateful. And I remember what you said - I make good with this, and you got other work for me. So I won't mess up. You think I want to lose that opportunity? So I won't, I won't. I'm being careful, I'm being polite, extra polite to everybody.

Well yeah, I know polite don't always work. I admit that. In T.O. I had a few bad ones - hotels mainly, I don't like working hotels, I'm glad you don't want me to do that. I'm comfortable with the way it is. Going well so far. I *appreciate* working with you, you know that. Glad to have your advice - your experience. And I'm glad to be here, eh! Don't miss T.O. at all.

So this guy today - he was a talker! Number Three. Lucky Three. Yeah, the one I was starting to tell you about. Remember, I said I gave him the usual spiel when he called - when we started talking, eh? Said he'd call back, and he did, couple days later. But it's funny - that's why I'm telling you about him. He knew a guy we both knew, Inside - how could we forget! Marv! Remember Marv! The Mighty Marvel, I called him? Yeah, the pedophile. That one. They soon moved him, I guess they saw what could happen to him on that range - they must of known Harvey hated them, pedophiles, on account of his father abusing him. Remember Happy Harvey? Always said he'd kill any one of us if he found we was bent that way, he wanted to rid the world of scum like that. Didn't mind fags, he said, if they kept out of his way, but he hated pedophiles. I saw Marv while Harvey was saying that - it was on the day he arrived - and he was pissing himself, what a cow! But he was a nice guy, sort of soft and hopeful and helpless, like pedophiles often are - with other guys, I mean, not with kids. So I told him I'd watch his back and he better keep very quiet. And I tell him he can do something for me. And for himself. See, he needed money for things, he didn't have no toothpaste and stuff, and I needed dollars to pay Herb - he was hanging free, see, and he told me he had to have it before he got out, he owed Harvey for smokes. So - all right, all right, I'm getting to the point. I am. Thought you'd be interested. Yeah, it *is* connected with Number Three. You'll see. It is. Right?

He was very nervous, Number Three. His first time, he said. I tried to calm him down but he just talked and talked and talked - what a talker! How he didn't know what to do because it was his first time so I must tell him and he had this sore back, he had twisted it playing ball with his son, and how he thought massage might help and he just happened to see my advert, it was the first time he had picked up "that free paper" he called it, *View*, he saw it as he came out of the drugstore, and how he liked the sound of my name. See, he liked the sound of my name! He liked the name. Brad. And he just went on and on. And he said a friend of his had been to the Tina Turner show and had I been to it? - No - Did I know anyone who *had* been to it? - No. And then somehow I knew who this guy was - see, I knew he lived in Hamilton, Marv said so, and I was there when he called him, and I guess I even maybe remembered his voice a bit, it was faint but I could hear it, I was standing right by Marv when he called the guy, he was an old friend, Marv said.

See, what happened, when I told Marv about the Tina Turner show, I said did Marv have anyone, family, or a friend, who could buy me a ticket for the show? 'Cause one of the guys said T.T. was coming to T.O. on her farewell tour, couple weeks after I would get out - yeah, I was hanging free then too, almost. So I said he should get someone outside to buy me a ticket, just a ticket for me, and send it to my mother, and I would give him fifty dollars credit for him to buy things. And see, that's what happened. He was grateful. Said he would never forget my kindness. And - here is his friend who bought the ticket, right here!

"So what?" Hey, it's only a story. 'Course I'm not trying to waste your time. Why would I do that? Thought you'd be interested, enjoy the story. And you know what, this guy, Number Three, he was real grateful too - like Marv. Couldn't stop thanking me. Never had it like that before, he said. He even - No, I mean he *offered* to pay me fifty. But I wouldn't take it. Said I was glad he had enjoyed it so much and he knew where I live now. He'll be back

Yeah, he did give me a name. Desmond Burton - but that for sure ain't his real name - it's not in the phonebook - but I got his number - yeah, you know, the answering-machine.You recording all this conversation?

No, I agree! Yeah, I know how they mostly give false names -

Right, right - I know you busy. Don't want to waste your time. Thanks for the conversation, eh! It's like in jail, when we first met, but *you* did most of the talking then, eh! You helped me get a grip on myself, you helped me. Hey, I'm grateful - real grateful, for everything. I won't forget, never. I wish you could of come over tonight. Hope you can come over soon, eh, when you not so busy. Just call me before to be sure I'm not at work!

Yeah, you was always there for me, in jail, I know it, and now too - and I'll always be there for you. That's a promise. I'll never forget!

Hey, you know, the view's good from here! I'm looking at it right now. Especially at night, it's a great view. All those lights shining in the darkness. You can see Stelco and Dofasco, and the jail of course, Barton Street, and the Lake, sort of. It's real dark out there, black, with the snow falling, just little specks of snow now but TV says lots more later tonight, big storm coming in from the States, eh - it's bad down there, Buffalo, that's what they're saying. And you can see the chimneys, the smoke-stacks, is that the right word? - and flames jumping up out of two of them, bright, bright in the darkness. Flames. From the furnaces - my father worked there, did I tell you that? At Stelco? Fire in the night, like in war movies, eh!

You still there? No, I'm not going on talking for ever! Used to say you liked to hear me talk, when we was Inside, remember? Said I cheered you up. You changed your mind now? Don't like me any more? But I still love you, eh. You're, like, my father, know that? I never knew my father. There was this old guy, he said he was my father, but Ma said good riddance when he went away and he was nothing but a liar and a drunkard, that's what she called him, and she said he couldn't even get it up. My real father died in a accident, she said, he was crushed one night by a load of steel bars, she said, even before I was born, he didn't have a chance. They were married. She used to take the ring off of her finger and let me hold it, or turn it round and round on her finger, I really liked to do that, don't know why. She said it was valuable, "my precious ring, it's all I have left of him" she used to say. That other one, the old guy, he wasn't my father and he wasn't her husband, they never married. He was just a drunkard, that's what she said, a no-good. Never kept a job for long, all his money went straight into booze, that's why we was dirt-poor, that's what she said. Because my father got crushed to death by a load of steel bars, in the darkness. Right here in Hamilton, right where I'm looking now, those flames in the darkness.

Yeah, I know I told you some of this, Inside. I remember that, eh! Yeah, 'course I do. But I didn't tell you all what I told you now, did I? And all about the ring? I never told you about the ring, did I? Never remembered it till now. It was a - I never saw a wedding-ring like that one! It was sort of silvery with black - dolphins I think she said they were called - like, big fish, three big fish swimming round and round. I wonder what happened to it? It wasn't on her finger when she died, I went to see her in hospital - they let me out of jail to visit her when she sent for me, she knew she was dying, that was just before I met you, my back was still hurting - but it was too late, she couldn't talk, didn't even open her eyes when I said "Ma, I'm here", but the nurse said to hold her hand so I did, and then she died. She said it was valuable, I wonder if one of the nurses stole it? She said my father bought it for her in one of those big fancy jewelry stores in T.O., but I seen rings like that on Yonge Street - you know, those little sidewalk stores.

Yeah, well all right, I'm sorry. Taking up your valuable time! "Gabbing"? What sort of word is that? I never heard that one before. "Gabbing"! Why do you say that? But hey - you know, you really are, like, my father now. You done so much for me already, and I know it's just the start, like you say. I hope you know I'm real grateful. I respect you. I do. I never respected a man before like I respect you. No, that's true. It's true. I don't lie no more.

So could you put that money in the account tomorrow? Thanks. No, I won't waste it, I promise. What would I spend it *on*? Hey? I only need it for food and some new clothes. When you come, you'll be proud of me in my new clothes - I want you to be proud of me, always. Proud to know me. Like I'm your son. Like *I'm* proud to know *you*, and always will be. So, look after yourself.

Oh, one thing I forgot about Number Three. He never knew I was the one he bought those tickets for, when I was Inside, but he would of if I wasn't Brad now, I mean if I still called myself what they called me when I was Inside. He said "I wonder what Tiger thought of Tina Turner, I hope he enjoyed it", and I said yeah, I was sure he did enjoy it, anybody would, and I know *I* would of enjoyed it. And I *would* of enjoyed it, 'course I would of. But I sold the tickets - the ticket - to a guy outside, you know, a scalper - the show was sold out.

Yeah, thanks, I will. Talk to you soon, eh. And *you* look after *your-self*, eh!

FOUR
Love is Doing

I don't mind talking about it all now. The tape-recorder? No problem - that's the way you do it, I know that. You can record everything
I say. I wouldn't talk when they came and shoved, like, mikes and
tape-recorders and movie-cameras and stuff in my face when I was
coming out of hospital - that was gross, I screamed at them, I'm, like,
Fuck off and leave me alone!

But I don't mind now. When I got your first letter, I wasn't ready?
So I didn't reply. Then your second letter came, and I'm, like, Maybe?
But I still didn't reply. Then when you called last week I knew I had to
do it, and now I could do it, I knew that - I *can* do it. Not for myself
and the money - that will be great, for me and Samantha, we don't got
much - single mother, no job, welfare don't go far these days? But for
Eric. I want to do it for him, and to try and make things better for other
kids - *if* they can ever be better?

Sometimes I think it'll always be bad for kids. If they get born in
poor families? If their parents don't love them and care for them? If
they get into trouble at school? Bullied, bad friends? Whatever. Lots
of things can go wrong, and if they start wrong - well, kids don't get a
second chance, do they? Know what I mean? You're only a child once.
And then they grow into bad grown-ups, and then it just goes on and
on? That's what I think. We got to change that. Got to do better for
them. Because, like, we was all kids, eh? - know what I mean? *I* was,
you was - and kids grow up, most of them anyways, the lucky ones, but

20

sometimes it might even be better if they die, eh? And things won't get better for any of us if they don't get better for kids first? That's what I think.

So I'll tell you all I can remember? I want to do that now. And it's Summer, and that makes it better, eh? Easier. It was Winter when all that happened to us, January, six months ago - those things about us that you know about, everybody knows about? And it was a bad winter, too - remember? So much snow, so many grey days? But now it's Summer. See that rose outside the window, with that pink flower, it just opened, it's called Peace - it was planted by Samantha's grandmother, on her birthday - *Samantha's* birthday I mean, her third.

I hope you'll make a true story out of what I tell you? I know you got to write it up, make it, like, more interesting for your readers? That's what every magazine and newspaper does? But no lies, please no lies, eh? I been reading your magazine, bought it in the drugstore, so's I could decide if I wanted Eric to be in it? But I hope you will tell it how it is, the whole thing - I mean, how it *was*. I hope you'll make it, like, the truth? I hope you won't be mean to us? Even to Derek? I hope you'll remember that he was Samantha's father, and one day she's going to read what you write. What you put in your magazine? Please remember that. Even if I don't show it to her, some other kid will, I know that. So please remember?

I made some notes, so's I don't forget some things, and so's I get things, like, in the right order? But I'm just going to talk first, just like talking to Eric, because I'm feeling nervous, and you can interrupt and ask me questions. Right?

I'll start about Marv and all that, I been thinking about him and what happened then, he was Derek's friend, it was two years ago, nearly - Eric was nine - when I went to visit my sister Sheila in Guelph. I lied about that? I said she was a friend, that's what I told the children? And I told Marv that too. See, she was, like, a junkie, my sister? I didn't want Eric and Samantha to know that, I decided that I would never ever tell them, so please don't put it in. An aunt who's a junkie! But when they called to say she was in hospital - I thought she was still in jail, see - and they said she was, like, calling for me, "crying out for you" they said, and she was dying they said - well, so I had to go. What they didn't tell me, she had AIDS too? She was dying of AIDS? *She* told me that.

So then I went. Just for the weekend, by bus, that's how long it was supposed to be, but it wasn't even that long? I got called back. See, I said the children could go with Marv, he wanted to take them camping for Samantha's birthday, and I had no idea. That he was a pedophile? I had no idea. That's why they called me back, the police did? They're, like, "We have apprehended the man, Marvin Mercier, who was with your children." An officer came, I was with Sheila, I was sitting there holding her hand, and she was trying to talk to me, and they called me away, they found me there because I left the hospital's phone number with Eric, just so's if there was any bad problem they could call me. "One of the other campers got suspicious when she saw Mercier on his own with the children. She asked the little girl, when she got the chance, when she was on her own in the washroom, you know, if the man was her father, and when she said no, and that her Mummy had gone away for the weekend, she called us, this camper did. Marvin Mercier is a convicted pedophile. He was breaking the conditions of his release, which stipulated that he should not at any time be in the company of children under sixteen."

Well, that isn't *exactly* what they said to me, I guess? - I copied some of this from the newspaper article - you know, about Marv's trial - and I'm, like, crying and shaking, but they said these things, they told me about Marv? They said they could drive me back to Hamilton but I didn't want that, don't know why - wanted to be on my own, I guess. So they put me on the first bus back to Hamilton - gave me some money too, so's I could buy sandwiches to eat on the way, the policewoman was kind. And I was so worried about the children? All the way. If he had done anything to them? All the way I cried and cried, about them and about leaving my sister like that - I never saw her again. She died four days after.

Then later there was all the stuff at the trial, all the publicity. Having to tell about the whole thing and answer, like, the lawyer's questions, and the judge and the jury, and the crowd in there watching and listening, and then reporters and stuff after. It was - gross, it was gross. And Marv there, in a red prison overall, so thin and sick, not looking at us, and me trying to not look at him? - and Eric, too, having to answer questions, testify, that's the word? - and people looking at me afterwards as if, like, as if I was the worst mother in the world, to let my children be with a pedophile? But I didn't *know* he was a pedophile, nobody told me. I was, like, "If I had of *known*" but nobody listened. He was just a very nice friendly helpful guy? And he was Derek's friend too. And I liked him, eh, I really liked him, and the children *loved* him? - Eric specially loved him, and even after all that, he won't let anyone say anything against Marv.

Yeah, he's still Inside, Marv - Warkworth, I think, now, for a few more months anyways - he was in Barton Street Jail first - Hamilton-Wentworth Detention Centre is its proper name I think, you would know - until after the trial - that's where my brother Stan was when I came to Hamilton four years ago, I came here partly because of that, like, to visit him - he was in for stealing things and for drugs, trafficking in drugs? I was the only one who visited him, my sister couldn't, she was pregnant and sick, and I guess she was already into drugs too - and my other brother, Dave, he wouldn't. My Dad and Mom are still alive, but I don't see them, don't want to see them, not *ever*. No, but - You don't want to hear about *me*, do you - my family and - whatever? Yes, I know you can leave it all out anyways, when you do the article, and I guess what happened to me, and Dave and Sheila and Stan, and Derek too - I guess that's also about what happens to kids in our society, how they get messed up and then they mess up other kids - even their own kids - specially their own kids, eh?

So, we grew up on a farm, near Walkerton? Yeah, Walkerton, everyone knows Walkerton now after that E. coli stuff, the poisoned water and deaths and sickness and stuff. But when we was growing up it was just the town where we did our shopping, went to school, got beaten up by the kids there. We was the Bentley brats, four of us - we was dirt-poor, clothes from the Amity - the Walkerton kids throwed snowballs and stones at us, my brothers got into fights, we dreaded if the school-bus was late. But it was worse at home. You don't want to know about it! My Dad, he was a drunk? - and a bully? - he made Dave and Stan do all the dirty work, feed the cattle, clean out the pig-styes, all that? - and he would come home drunk and he would beat Dave, he would be screaming, like, "You stupid fuckin cunt, you no-good fuckin bastard", and we could hear him beating Dave, and we would sit very quiet, Sheila and me, and hope he wouldn't notice us, and then we'd creep upstairs to bed when we got the chance? - and we'd hear him still screaming and beating Dave, and then he'd fall down or lie down on the sofa and after a while you'd hear him snoring and Dave would creep up the stairs and look in to see if we was all right and he'd be trying not to let us see he was still crying and shaking and - I guess it's good that Dave ran away, and stayed away, when he was seventeen, and now he's married and he's got a good job, manager of a Tim Horton's, and his wife won't let him even talk to us. I was angry with her at first, but now I think she's right, they got no children but maybe they will and she's got to think of them first, and herself and Dave too, and her family, they didn't want her to marry Dave, eh? He would help us, any of us, I know he would, if she gave him the chance? - but she makes sure he stays on the right path, no boozing with the guys after work, all his money goes to her, and they go to church on Sunday. That's what Sheila says - she went to the Tim Horton's and made him talk to her, she's like that - she's the feisty one - I was the quiet one, the timid one. I guess he's happy - I hope so. The only one of us four who didn't get into drugs or alcohol?

My mother? Oh, she went away even before Dave did. Dad used to beat her up too. She was a pill-popper, know what I mean? They was all over the house, her sleeping-pills and stuff. When we'd come home from school, most of the time there was no meal cooked, nothing, and the house was filthy - dirty, smelt almost as bad as the pig-styes? And she'd be in bed with the door closed? Once I got friendly with a Walkerton girl at school and she wanted to visit, said she loved being on a farm, loved animals, and so that was the end of the friendship - I wasn't going to let any of them kids see our place! Anyways, one day we come home from school - I think I was eleven then, I was the youngest? - and she's gone, didn't even leave a note. Sheila found out where she was, later - she was living with another man, some farmer she met at the market, I think? - on a farm way on the other side of Mount Forest? But I never wanted to see her again. She left us, just like that, she didn't even care what happened to us, she left us with that man? My father! *She* was bad enough, but *he* was worse. I hated him. You wouldn't want to know what he did to me.

No. I won't tell. But it was bad. It was real bad. Then I got - I got that I hated all men, all males? - for a while. Derek was another one, violent, when he was drunk? Only Marv wasn't violent, ever. But Derek said Marv wasn't really a man, he was, like, a woman inside a man's body? - that's what he said. See, I got to know Marv because he was a friend of Derek's, sort of? - they got to be friends in jail, Derek protected Marv, he said - you know, because he was, like, a queer - yes, gay, that's it - and he could of been killed, they hate gays in jail?

Derek? I met Derek at Sheila's - she was having her second baby, and her boyfriend had left her, Jeff, so I said I would come and, like, keep house for a while, till she was strong - and look after her first, Brittany, she was just one, a year younger than Eric, almost? - and Derek was a friend of the guy next-door, who was, like, keen on Sheila, that's why her boyfriend left, he found them together? - he did skate-boarding and snow-boarding with Derek, this guy next-door did. I fell in love with Derek, he was a real handsome guy in those days, and could he talk! Everybody was his friend when he was like that! Made me laugh and laugh with his jokes and cheek, eh? But he could be real quiet too and just go on long walks, he wouldn't let me come, "Moody" my sister said "and moody means trouble". But I didn't care, I thought he was exciting, you never knew what he was thinking, you never knew what he would say next, what he would do next. He was twenty-three, I think - I was twenty-two. I didn't know he was an alcoholic. You'd think I'd be an expert on that, eh, what with my father? But I didn't know. And of course he knew how to cover it up, eh? Started drinking when he was a kid, he told me that later, just fifteen I think he said, some of his skateboarding buddies, they were rich Westdale kids and they would steal, like, whisky and stuff from their parents. I was grateful, too, that he didn't mind about Eric - he'd play games with Eric, he was six, even taught him how to ride a bike, how to do skateboarding, so they got on real well at first - I wanted him to have a father too, and Derek's, like, "I don't mind, so long as I get to have a son of my own later"? And he said "Derek and Eric, Derek and Eric - what a team! Sounds like one of those comedy acts, like Wayne and Schuster - we was meant to be together!" So I moved in with him, Eric and me did, after Sheila was all right - he had a nice apartment in Stoney Creek then? - and I was happy with him for a year, and Samantha was born and -

But then everything went wrong? He was drinking more and more, though he always swore not - he'd come home late, after work, he was working at Stelco then? - and he'd been drinking with the guys and he'd be smelling of whisky, and there was hardly any money for food and clothes, and he'd get abusive even if I said nothing, and he'd hit me, just suddenly slap me about, "Why are you looking at me like that, who do you think you are?" and he even knocked me down, banged my head on the floor, twice he did that, gave me a black eye too, but he said sorry next day and he would never do that again? But then he hit Eric, and after that I told him I'd leave him if he he ever did that again, and when he did I took the children while he was asleep and went to a shelter, but I didn't like it there, and the children hated it? So after a while I went back and he promised me he'd never drink again, but he did, and - Whatever. You know how it is.

So I was just another Battered Woman - that's what they told me in the shelter, eh? - they told me to have, like, pride in myself as a woman, be sensible, "Never let a man do that to you, never tolerate violence by anyone, never to go back after", but I did. He had other women, too, I knew that - I could smell it on him? Then he got caught by the police and turned out he'd been selling drugs, and he had been let go at Dofasco and he never told me - he was getting money from selling the drugs, he was a crack-dealer I guess, so he was in jail for more than a year, and I said it was over between us, but he begged me not to leave him, he's, like, "Wait for me, please wait for me, I've learnt my lesson, I'll never touch another drink, I'll never have anything to do with drugs, I'll never hurt you again, never, never, I promise"? - and I was weak again, I sent him money and visited him there, OCI - I even took the children in there which I never should of, eh? Stupid, stupid, wasn't I? I used to tell myself that all the time, "You stupid stupid *stupid* bitch!" - but I couldn't turn my back on him, just couldn't, I loved him. Loved him. Know what I mean?

And also I was sorry for him? See, he had a bad childhood, too, like me - worse, it was even worse than mine, if he was telling the truth, but sometimes, like, I wondered if he *was*. He said he never had no father? - and his stepfather beat him, and his mother abandoned him, like our mother did? He said. But when he was in jail the second time, for getting drunk and trying to break into an LCBO when he was still on probation - I wasn't there, we had been living in a basement apartment in the East End - Wentworth North - but I got away and I was in another shelter with the two children? - see, he knocked me down again, two nights before, and my right arm was hurting bad and I was frightened he would hurt the children real bad, so - His mother came to see me? Said his lawyer had phoned her to find out some things about Derek, and he told her about me, and also she knew one of the women running the shelter I was in. So she came to see us there and she seemed a nice lady, said she hadn't seen Derek for years, he ran away and she didn't know where he was till the lawyer phoned, he wanted more information to help in what he would say. So then she helped me, and she loved Eric and Samantha, "My beautiful little grandchildren", and they liked her too, she would spoil them with presents, she came to see us almost every day but her health was bad, her heart, she's dead now, eh? - but she made me wonder if what Derek told me was the truth. But it was the children I was worried about, and when he would come out again and move in with us? - see, he didn't have nowhere else to go, except a lodging-home. So his mother helped me while he was back in jail, she gave me some money, and helped me get this apartment, here in West Hamilton, and move into it, and helped me get furniture too, and helped with the rent, and Eric was happy in the school here? - he was getting good grades, his teacher said he was smart, real smart. So I thought things would work out good this time.

I wrote Derek, he was in Maplehurst then, and told him all about it, and about his Mom and how she was helping us and how she wanted to see him? - and how she said we would be a real family when he came out, with a nice place and all. She said to me "He'll have so much to live for, he'll be so happy with you and the children, he'll never drink again with so much to lose." But he got drunk the second night he was out, and kicked in a restaurant window, just went out in the middle of the night, I tried to stop him but - So he was back inside, third time, before his Mom could even see him. So then I told her it couldn't work and it would be better if we didn't see each other any more and I would be going away - I thought I would go right away where he couldn't find me, out West? She was very upset, and then, before I could go - I was waiting for the end of the school-term - she had another heart-attack, last November it was, and she was in hospital after that, and she begged me to wait till she was better, so's we could talk and so's she could have some time with the children before we left. So I did? And also it was getting near Christmas, so I didn't want to take the children away then from the friends they had here, and all that - you know how it is? Stupid, stupid, stupid - always *stupid*! But I didn't visit her, and I didn't want the children to be with her again, not till I knew if we would stay in Hamilton, but I called her sometimes and we would talk, and sometimes she called me from hospital. She said she needed to see Derek, so badly, she needed to talk to him, and everything would be all right for all of us, she knew it would be - and she made me promise to take him straight to her when he came out, to the hospital.

So then he came out, and - You know what happened after that. It was in all the newspapers, on TV, everywhere. It was so - horrible, horrible. See, I promised myself I would never let Eric and Samantha suffer anything like what I did, and my sister and brothers - I would always protect them, always, always and - Just see what - So I hated myself at first, eh? I didn't do it to Eric, but for the longest time it seemed like I did. If I had gone away before Christmas, if I hadn't fallen in love with Derek, if I had left him long ago - Oh, if, if, if, if! And how I would lie there in the hospital after they told me what happened and I'm thinking over and over, Why him, why not me, why Eric? I was the one should have died, not him, and I deserved to die too, for some of the things I done. And I'm thinking, like, Let me die now, please let me die, I want to die, I just want to die. But then after a while I'm thinking I must be alive for Samantha. One of the neighbours was looking after her, and they brought her to see me, and she just put her arms round my neck, and then I knew I was saved for *her*. See, Eric always tried to protect her, if the other children teased her or hit her, they loved each other so much and he would protect her - like he tried to protect me too. But he was only a child himself still, he was only eleven years old, he couldn't do it all and now he's gone. So that's why, eh? I got to do what he wanted, and one night it's like I was woken up, in hospital, and I'm, like, hearing his voice and he's saying "You got to look after her for me, Mom - Sam needs you, Mom", he always called her Sam. So that's why. I got to do that for him, I got to protect Samantha, I got to live for her. And I will. For Eric.

His father? Eric's? Eric's father? I know what you'll think? You'll think I am a real slut when I say I don't know who Eric's father is. See - All right, you really want to know? All right, then I'll tell you. For the longest time I thought it was, like, my fault, I felt so ashamed - but it wasn't, the counselor in the shelter said so too. My father would, like - he would have sex with me - with my sister too, before me, she told me about that later, said she felt guilty because she was happy when he stopped with her and started with me, she was a year older than me - And see, one night he brought home some guy he knew, and they both did it to me. And the next week - There were two older boys at school, they had been, like, teasing me and following me and laughing at me, they came on the school bus, they were farm-boys, and my sister would walk home with me - Dave was gone by then, and Stan had finished school, he was seventeen, he had a job in a garage pumping gas, he was away all day and half the night too - or maybe he had already gone to Toronto, he was a squeegee-kid there, that's how he got into drugs? And that day, Sheila was sick and I went to school on my own, and on the way home the two boys stayed on the bus and got off when I did - the driver talked to them and asked them why, what were they doing, I think she was worried, but they just cheeked her and she drove on, and so then - I don't want to tell you this. I think you can guess what happened. It was getting dark? I walked fast along the track, trying to get ahead of them, but they followed close behind, they were, like, laughing and saying I was a slut and whatever, saying all the guys talked about fucking me - so then they grabbed me when we came near a barn and I screamed but they put their hands over my mouth and dragged me inside -

Fifteen, I was fifteen. So. Now you know why I don't know who Eric's father is? Anyone of those four could of been his father! And when my father knew I was pregnant, he wanted to throw me out, said I was a disgrace to him and the whole family and I should get an abortion, that's all he would pay for, and if I said anything about him and me he would kill me, he would come and find me, wherever I went, and kill me? - So I dropped out of school, and Sheila did too, she said we would stay together, she would look after me - and she did, and the baby was born. She found an apartment for us in Walkerton, she got work in a store there and she got money from Dave too, she went to the Tim Horton's and told him what happened - then she took me to the hospital by taxi when my labour started - So. Eric was born. He was an easy child, no problems - not like Samantha! We both loved him, Sheila and me. And I got a part-time job at the same store as Sheila. But - See, I wondered if Eric was cursed - if he was, like, my father's son - because that would be wrong, wouldn't it? Evil - wouldn't it be evil? That's in the Bible, isn't it? See, he looked like me, everyone said so - but one of those boys had fair hair, too, Randy, like my father? - and Eric looks like him too, sort of. So - Randy could of been the father? But I always wondered if he was my father's son and was he cursed by God? I still wonder about that.

Then Sheila met this guy, and he was from Hamilton, Jeff, so she moved in with him there, in the North End, Wentworth, like I said? And she said, like, I could live with her and Jeff, and also Stan was in jail there, Barton Street? - he was just arrested and waiting for his trial and he wanted us to visit and bring him some money for canteen, for cigarettes - he phoned Dave but his wife wouldn't let him go, so he told Sheila. Anyways, I did go with Sheila to Hamilton, I wanted to get away from Walkerton, far away from my father - but Jeff didn't want us around, Eric and me, I could see that, and he complained, "No privacy, can't hear myself think", and Sheila got pregnant, and so then I found my own place nearby, just one room - I was on welfare then, while Eric was small?- Yeah, I told you about how Jeff left Sheila anyways, and how I got to know Derek and whatever? And Sheila, I told you about her. But I don't know how she got into drugs, crack I think, she started after her second child was born, Brandon - I think that guy next-door, Derek's friend, she moved in with him and he was a crack-head. So, after Jeff left, and me too, both of the children were taken away from her by Children's Aid - the baby nearly died, the boyfriend took it to the hospital, it was round the corner, the General, and it nearly died there - she didn't feed it, they said, she wasn't a fit mother, they said, and both her kids, they was put out for adoption, in Toronto. So she went there, didn't even tell me she was going, I was living with Derek in Stoney Creek by then, I was pregnant with Samantha, and she got into - she was a prostitute, they said - she became a prostitute in Toronto, to pay for drugs - a junkie, she was a junkie by then. I tried to find her twice but I couldn't, I think even Dave didn't know where she was, I think she didn't want any of us to know, and Stan tried to find her too, after he came out, but she never called any of us, not till she was dying.

So. I guess I told you everything I can remember, eh?

No, I can't say I'm *happy* here - but maybe content now, sort of, Samantha and me, in this apartment. In Hamilton. Got friends, eh? At first I thought I couldn't stay here, after such terrible things, I couldn't bear the memories and you think everybody's looking at you and talking about you. But then I did stay - didn't have nowhere else to go, and I was - I just felt so tired then, after I came out of the hospital, so weak and sick. And most of the neighbours, even the ones who complained and looked down their noses at us, they been kind - one lady, the one who bugged me about their clothes, she looked after Samantha and now she's, like, a grandmother to her, and another one brought pizzas and fruit and stuff when I came out. I guess most of them just feel sorry for us, but I don't mind. I'm glad I stayed - thought I would leave soon as I felt better, soon as Spring came - go West, whatever, like I wanted before. But I didn't go before, when I could of - things would have been different, real different, if I'd went then, eh! But I didn't, and now I'm glad I didn't. There's a guy here too, he's divorced, he wants to marry me - he's kind, gentle, a sweet guy - a real gentleman, Keith. He's from the Islands, Trinidad. He loves Samantha too, he's like a father to her. Also another guy, he came to see me after he read about us in the *Spec* and he gave me money to pay the rent, I said No, but he, like, insisted, said anytime I need help I just phone him. So. I'll see what happens, but I'm content, like I say - well, I'm sad about all what happened, course I am - but then I look at Samantha and I think, so much suffering, so many bad things, but look at her laughing and running around and playing and - I just want her life to be happy. I just want her to be happy. Know what I mean?

So that's all I got to say. I already said way too much, eh! Way too much! Unless you got any more questions?

Yeah, well I guess I should of. They told me that in the shelters too - that he was evil, "a dangerous destructive man, a sexual predator" they said - abuse, incest, he could hurt more people, specially women and children, and anyways he should be punished for what he did to his wife and children, he should be put away, whatever - I should go to the police - they even got the police to visit me and, like, ask questions about what happened, and *they* said I should charge him too. And even the other guy and those two boys - grown men now, those two should be charged too. But I wouldn't? Don't know why. I wouldn't and I won't. Yeah, I do think he's still alive. I think Dave would tell me if he died - Dave knows where I am, here - he paid for Sheila's funeral, and he wrote me and sent a photo of the grave.

But he'll be all alone now, my father - no family, he's got rid of us all, and he's getting old and he'll die alone, all alone, in that stirking farmhouse - so he'll suffer enough, eh? And his guilty conscience too? He's just a sad old man now. That's what I think. I don't want to see him again, I don't want him to come near Samantha, but I don't hate him, I don't. And he was just a coward, anyways. He hurt us because he was hurting inside, maybe - maybe *his* father abused him, yes I think that's how it maybe was, and he was so angry inside, and we was weaker than him and so he could make *us* suffer too, for what his father did to him? So I won't. I won't. He's my father, and see, you got to try to forgive and forget, eh? If you don't forgive sometime, you can't forget, that's what I think. You got to move on, no use blaming anyone, just do your best. Know what I mean?

See, I don't want any more suffering, I hate it, violence and suffering, violence and suffering - everywhere you look, on television too, people hurting each other, violence and suffering, but if you hurt other people, like he did, then you hurt yourself too. And it just goes on, the violence and suffering. All of us, eh? We're all like that? I hope you'll say that in the article? For Eric and me and Samantha and Sheila. Yeah, and Dave and Stan. And Derek too. Yes, Derek too. And all the kids who get abused, everywhere. You hear people talking about love, eh? - how we should love each other, and how the Bible says we must, Jesus says we must, specially the weak and helpless, specially kids, eh? - we must love them most of all. Hey, but love isn't just talking, love is *doing*. Know what I mean? Not talking about it, not reading about it, not listening about it, not thinking about it - *doing* it. Love is *doing*. That's what I think.

FIVE
A Cloud of Witnesses

No, I didn't see or hear anything unusual earlier that day. The two children were out playing in the snow that morning, it was a Saturday - though they were often home from school - I remember seeing them out there - I think they were making a snowman - it's been quite an industry here, Inspector - is it Inspector? No? Look, you can see that one there. It seems wrong somehow, doesn't it, to see it still standing there, with that silly red hat and that big smile. And other snowmen that the kids round here made have been knocked down. It's been such a good winter for kids, so much snow, all the local kids have been having a ball. But lots of fighting too! Gangs running around throwing snowballs at each other - noise, noise, I don't mind kids' noise, it's only natural, as long as it's not excessive, but some of the adults in these apartments got very annoyed - the ones that do shift-work, they didn't exactly enjoy being woken up by shrieking kids! I went out a few times myself, to tell them to be quieter, and I was worried that some of the little girls might get hurt -

Yes, sorry, I do talk, don't I? My husband says I do. Anyway, I did worry a bit about those two children. I don't like to talk ill of her now - They didn't have good winter clothes, or at least I didn't think so. I gave them coats and gloves my boys had grown out of, perfectly good still, much better than what they were wearing. But she wouldn't accept that, she sent them over next day with the coats, not a word of thanks, and she never spoke to me after that. I mean - I know what pride is,

I've had to struggle too, never had much to spare, and I grew up in poverty, but what I say is, you have to put the children first, you have to sacrifice your own feelings, however hard that may be - they come first. Anyway, I didn't resent it. But *she* seemed to and - I know she did try, she told me once - while she was still talking to me, I mean - that she had applied for jobs downtown, but, whether she did or not - people did say that she wasn't always, well, she wasn't always quite honest, and she seemed to owe money to everyone around here in the end - Anyway, she never did get any employment. Well - not during the day.

They lived on welfare, her and the kids, and - you know, some of these unmarried mothers don't exactly know how to spend money wisely, they get these handouts from the Government and spend it all in a few days - they buy things they don't really need, and expensive things for their kids, video-games and so on, and they gamble at the corner store, Lotto or whatever it's called, I don't hold with gambling in any form, it's a sin, but if you don't have enough money to feed your kids, well - She had pizzas delivered, I saw that often enough, night after night, instead of cooking them good food - I had them in sometimes, early on, after school, with my own two, and gave them supper, but she soon stopped that. She was - Well, it's only the truth to say she was a difficult young woman - over-sensitive, thought you were getting at her whenever you tried to help.

That evening? No, I didn't hear anything unusual before eight. There's always some noise here, you get used to it - you have to get used to it or you would never get any sleep. That's what my husband says. You hear kids screaming, and the parents too - screaming at each other often, even if you try not to hear. When I first came here I actually called the police one night, Inspector, and a policeman came and I had to give a statement, and the couple who had been fighting, it sounded as if he was killing her, she was screaming, screaming, and the banging and bumping, it was just above me - terrible, terrible! But they said it was all in play, just a game, and he believed them, your policeman - and those two spread vicious rumours about me after that, and people here thought I was a troublemaker. So I decided I would never do that again. Mind your own business! That's what my husband says. And I know there's drugs here too, in this building, you can smell marijuana in the passage sometimes, I know what that smells like. But I just try to ignore what goes on, Inspector. For a quiet life - or as quiet as it can ever be in a building like this.

No, I didn't see a strange man that afternoon. Or any man. Around five or six? No. And I didn't hear anything then or later, before the screaming. Probably I was watching TV, I usually do after dinner, after washing-up, I like to relax then. And my husband watches the CBC Sports every Saturday afternoon. At other times I did see some strange men around, but they might not have been for her. She did go out quite often at night, people said, and one night I woke up, it was in the early morning, I had to go to the bathroom, and I happened to look out of the front window and saw her getting out of a car - No, I don't know what sort of car, I don't know about cars, and it was too far away to see the driver. A big car, dark. Oh but there was also that man - you must know about that man, I forget his name, over a year ago I think it was, a while back anyway, who got friendly with them, apparently he was after the children, he was what do you call them, a pediophile? There was a lot of talk about that at the time, a lot of publicity. But he would be in prison still, that man - I remember he was sentenced to a few years in prison. Some people said they wondered if she had been responsible, if she had encouraged him, fancied him even - she should never have let the children go off with him on their own.

She wasn't - I'm sorry, I know one shouldn't speak ill of the dead - or the dying, they say she's not likely to recover, is that right? - but she wasn't a good mother, and that's only the truth. I think the little girl, Samantha, will be better off now , both the children will - I'll be honest - they'll get a better upbringing. If their mother dies, I mean. The child does cry out in the night for her mother, but children are resilient - she'll forget, get over it all soon - I'm sure she will. When she started screaming that night - just two nights ago, wasn't it, but already it seems so long ago - at around eight o'clock it was, my blood ran cold, Inspector. My husband ran down, we were watching TV, but the door was locked - the man must have pulled it behind him when he escaped and it locked - and the child was screaming and screaming, and then other people came - that black man down the passage who was often with them, fancied the mother I think, and that loud foreign woman who's always complaining - he tried to calm the child through the door, but none of us could get in, and the screaming and whimpering went on and on - the door was locked, and the windows too, my husband went outside to try to get in that way - it's a ground-floor apartment, a corner one, as you know, and I've seen the children climbing in and out the windows, but they were locked too and my husband couldn't open them. But then the police arrived - someone must have called 911 - and they broke the door down, and the mother and son were lying there on the floor, it was a horrible sight, I just caught a glimpse - so much blood, and no movement at all - they were just lying there like corpses.

But the little girl stopped screaming and ran towards us and I picked her up and hugged her and she just whimpered and whimpered.

No, I don't think she does know who did it - she was asleep, I think, when it happened, and didn't see the attack. But she is still so traumatized - that's what the psychiatrist said who came to see her, and she can't seem to talk yet, hasn't said a word, just looks at you - she just needs to stay in a calm environment until she gets over the shock - so that's what I'm doing, Inspector - the psychiatrist agreed - and she's asleep now, but she did eat better today. As I say, children are so resilient - one of my two boys was knocked down by a man on a bicycle when he was only three and banged his head on the sidewalk and I was terrified he would be permanently damaged, but he recovered completely in just a few days.

But it's all so very sad, Inspector, tragic. I hope you catch the man who did it soon and it's a pity we don't still have capital punishment, in my view - my husband feels the same way - a vicious murderer like that deserves to die - especially if it was the child's father - I never met him but apparently he's been in and out of prison for years, and he was here briefly some months ago and robbed a local store and was caught and sent back to jail, and one of our neighbors said he thought he would be coming out again soon, but she was so secretive, she never told anyone about that apparently - and he saw the two of them going into her apartment with the little girl, early on Friday afternoon I think it was - but he'll tell you that when you talk to him - you're interviewing everyone in these apartments, aren't you, Inspector?

Yes, as I say, it's so tragic, so very very tragic, Inspector. What is happening to our society? So much violence, no morals, no standards of behaviour now, that's -   But at least Samantha will have Eric - her brother - they say he will recover, he's not so badly hurt as his mother - so I hope I'll be able to take Samantha to see him soon in hospital. That will help them both, they were always together - if you ask me, they were closer to each other than to their mother - he's very protective, looks after her even when they're playing those noisy games with the other children!

He was a friendly guy. Almost too friendly, if you know what I mean.

Saw him almost every day, morning or evening, sometimes both. In the elevator. Going up or going down. His place - the penthouse apartment, don't they call it that, right on top? 14th floor but it's really 13th floor - well, as you see, I'm two below, 11th floor. So we would talk some. And could he talk! And joke. He'd crack me up sometimes. No, sorry, I never remember jokes. One of those silent backroom types women don't notice, if you know what I mean, that's me. No small-talk.

Oh, I remember one, I think it was the last time I saw him, why I remember it I guess - not exactly a joke, but I laughed. He just had that effect on me, he cracked me up just grinning at me. My name's Brown - you know that - Malcolm Brown, M.O.R. Brown, my initials - somehow I told him that, when we first talked, introduced ourselves you know. Yes, Brad Forrest, two R's, that was his name. So, that morning, he says "Hi, Pal" - always called me Pal - "Mr Malcolm Brown!" Oh, I should have said - but you noticed, coming up? - the elevator interior is brown, brown all around you, and he had said how gloomy, why were elevators usually so gloomy. So now he says, and he looks all round, and up and down, and all round again, he was quite a comic, "But which of you is more Brown?" Well, all right, don't seem funny now - especially when I tell it, I can't tell jokes. But it was funny then. Cracked me up. And I says "You tell me, you B.F.!" And he just looks at me, stares at me, and staggers back and puts his hand over his mouth and says "Hey, that's funny! You made a joke, Pal! You said you couldn't and you did! You did! Want to get together tonight and celebrate? We should celebrate!"

No, we never did get together. I know, that was the night. But I didn't even think about it till afterwards - a few days later, when - you know what I mean, it was in the papers, on TV, everywhere. See, he often said things like that - let's have a drink together, you must come up and see my place, told me he was a great cook and he'd have me to dinner soon, said he was having a party for a friend and he wanted me to meet him, and so on. Almost every time we talked. But it never happened. You didn't hear any more about it. Just more talk like that. At first I would wait for the phone to ring, or I'd think he would knock on my door, I would even be listening for a knock in case I missed it. Then I knew it didn't mean anything. Just his way of being friendly. Some people are like that. My wife - my ex-wife - she was like that, promises, promises, let's just wait till tomorrow night, honey. But to-morrow night never came. And that's not a joke!

So that's it. Anything else I can tell you? See, I didn't know him that well. Just elevator talk, if you see what I mean. Never got beyond that. Just because we would meet in the elevator, and often it would be just him and me, near the top at least, I guess that's why we would talk.

No, one of your men asked me that already - that night, after - he was found. Didn't see anything unusual, didn't hear anything unusual, that night. Didn't see any strange man. Guess I was watching television. I always watch the CBC news-headlines on "Newsworld" at eight and then go to bed. That's my life, early to bed, early to rise - I'm up at five, work out, then work hard all day, mind my own business.

It's a pleasure.

She was a bitch, that one, a fuckin bitch. One of those quiet bitches, those are the worst ones, for sure. All that stuff about being a good mother, really caring for her kids, some around here fell for that. But I didn't. She had a foul mouth, she would talk foul stuff, she would glare at you and talk foul, just quietly so nobody else could hear, like "Fuck off!" if you just said one word to her kids about making a noise - and I'll tell you, they made a noise! All the kids are noisy round here, but those two were the worst, especially the girl, screaming, yelling. All times of the day, too. They were always away from school, she said they were sick, but they were never too fuckin sick to shout and scream under my window! I got to get my fuckin sleep! I work for my living! Not like her. Always waiting for her welfare check so she could go out and spend it on drugs.

No, well, I can't swear to it. No, I never actually saw her shooting-up or anything. She just had that funny look in her eyes. But you should ask some of the others in this building. Ask the black guy in 5, he fancied her I think - he would visit her and play with the kids, throw ball for them, you couldn't say anything against her if he was around. But I'll tell you, sometimes you could smell weed in the passage - you know, that sweet smell. I don't smoke weed now, but when I was a kid - you know how it was, your friend would show you, you'd be at a party, we all did it. But like I say, I don't do it now. I'm married now, I'm a father, I'm not as fuckin young as I was, don't want to lose this job. And don't want my kids getting into drugs.

No, nothing else. Except - I'll tell you, but here again I got no proof, you know. But just because you asked. I think she was a whore too, a fuckin prostitute. I think she made money to pay for hash that way. She would be out at night, see. I come back from my shift and I see her, she's getting into some guy's car at two in the morning. What? It was a ways away, under the trees, but I'd say a dark-coloured Merc, something like that. Yeah, more than once I seen her doing that. Five times? So why you doing that unless you - She was a fuckin whore, musta been! Got what was coming to her, I'll tell you that. What was coming to her. For sure.

He seemed a very nice young man. Always smiling. But I did wonder about him a bit.

Well, we get some very pretty, well-dressed young women in here. Customers. They come in here for a quick lunch? Because we're near their work - those big buildings across the street? They're secretaries in the offices there? They also look for men, you know - I hear them talking, and you know how these young ones are today, sex, sex, sex? Just look at these television programmes, "Sex in New York", is that what it's called? And so many others. And movies? Women are just as bad as men today, I always say - no morals, just find a man and into bed with him? It's all because we have no morals - no expectations for our kids, no standards, education's just a mess, they do what they want when they want how they want? And marriage vows mean nothing now. Who wants to Love, Honor and Obey when you can pick up a boy-toy and have a night's fun with him, then goodbye the next morning? I see it in my own children, my own grandchildren - I've got five of them. I have to be careful not to say critical things, they just flare up. Mothers today, they even take small children to movies at night, leave them locked in cars while they play bingo? Remember that case of the baby who died of suffocation, her mother was playing bingo?

About him? Oh yes, that young man, I liked him, he was always polite, please and thank-you, and he would tell little jokes. Not many young men are like that now, you know? And he was lively, always smiling and looking at people.

A small man, but good-looking, muscular. But he was always on his own. He would just eat his soup and sandwich - or his all-day breakfast, he liked that, two sausages, peameal bacon, two eggs sunny-side-up, toast and jam - coffee - then he would pay and go. He always left a tip too, not a big one, but showed his appreciation? I liked that. You'd be surprised how many don't leave a tip, even when you've given them lots of extra service. And you know, I'd see some of the young women, quite a few of them in fact, I'd see them try to attract his attention, I'd see them talking about him, interested in him, you know? But it was as if he didn't even notice? But he must have noticed. Any normal young man would have noticed? That's what I mean, any normal young man would have noticed. A couple of times, even, a pretty young woman would sit down at his table - you know, saying "Excuse me but would you mind, there isn't another place?", when we were busy? And he was polite, but that was all, yes and no, no jokes, no chat? But he liked talking with older women like me. So I wondered.

Yes, I did get to know her quite well. But not *really* well. Nancy was a very private person.

Yes, I was romantically interested in her. She was a nice young woman.

No, I'm divorced. My wife left me for another man.

Yes, one child. My wife was awarded custody. My lawyer is fighting that. He thinks it may be racial prejudice. But I have the right to have my son for one day every two weeks. I pick him up and we spend the day together. Saturday. I took him to a movie and McDonald's for a treat that Saturday, last Saturday. That Grinch one - Jim Carrey.

Yes, I liked her children. Very lively. I got on well with them. Sometimes she asked me to keep an eye on them - well, just be available so Eric could call me if there were any problems. But there never were any problems. He is amazingly responsible for an eleven-year-old boy, and he always looked after Samantha very efficiently and kindly, and she adored him, did everything he said. Nancy asked me to look after them that day, but of course I couldn't as it was my day with Matthew. She probably asked one of the other neighbors.

Well - I think she was suspicious of men. She'd had some bad experiences. She hinted about that. And quite recently there had been an unfortunate incident when a man got friendly with her and the children, and then when she had to go away for the weekend he took them away and fortunately the police got there in time. She was very upset about that.

No, she didn't talk a lot about it. She didn't talk a lot about anything. As I say, she was a very private person. But she did tell me that the two children had different fathers. To explain, I think, why they look so different - the girl, Samantha, is dark, the boy, Eric, is quite fair. I understood that she had been married to the boy's father, but he died in an accident. And the girl's father turned out to be a chronic alcoholic, and violent. The little boy, Eric, said that the man used to hit his mother, and also hit the children, and was in jail.

Well, sometimes I could tell that she was jittery. I thought she might even be frightened. She wouldn't say why, if I tried to talk about it, but once Eric said that the man would be coming out of jail soon. So I put two and two together.

Yes, I did talk to her once about it. Sideways, as it were. I told her about a fictional friend of mine who had been abused by her husband for five years and he had sworn to kill her as soon as he got out of jail and how she had gone to a shelter, how they would take her and the children and give them help and protection, and how it saved this friend's life because her husband came after her to kill her when he got out.

She just smiled. She said she'd been in a shelter before and she didn't like it. She said she was all right. And the children. Her situation wasn't like my friend's. I don't think she thought they were in any danger. And anyway, she had friends like me, she said. So she'd be all right, and the children too. That I shouldn't worry. And look what happened! Look what happened.

No, I'm sorry, I can't say any more, I can't give any help, I wish I could. I wish I could have helped her. And the children. Excuse me. I have to prepare for a class. Yes, I teach at the University.

Oh, come in, Officer. Let's go through to the sitting-room - I've got a fire going, so you'll be able to warm up a bit. So much snow this winter! Would you like a coffee? I'm just about to have one.

No, I didn't know him. He was pretty reclusive, you know. I'd see him driving past my gates quite often, but I spoke to him only once or twice in all the years. When he moved in - that would have been five years ago - I walked over to introduce myself, and we had a chat at his front door. Didn't invite me in, said very little, no personal information. "My name's McGregor" and that was about all. I said he'd be welcome to come over here and have coffee or a drink with us, almost any time - my wife was still alive then; but he never did, and he never invited us over. So after a while we just accepted that he didn't want anything to do with his neighbours, just keep to himself; this is, after all a quiet neighbourhood - an "exclusive" neighbourhood - and a lot of the people here value their privacy, don't want to be bothered with requests for money and so on; so his reticence wasn't surprising, and, to be honest, it didn't bother me at all - I was very busy in those days, to and from Toronto every day, and I didn't have a whole lot of time at home, until I gave it all up. Yes, he moved in when I was still in Government; two years before I retired.

No, I'm sure there was no wife, or any other women - we'd have noticed that!

Well, you can see that these houses are pretty far apart, and, with

all the trees between us as well, I wouldn't have been able to see much going on there even if I'd wanted to. Mostly, I think, there was nothing going on - no parties, no noise; in fact, we worried more about disturbing *his* peace and quiet. Our barking dog, occasional dinner-parties, etcetera.

Yes, I think there were visitors occasionally - you'd see a stretch-limo or two in his driveway; but I didn't pay any close attention. Mostly I noticed when I walked past taking our dog for a walk in the evenings. I did know of course that he had two cars of his own, and that struck me as an interesting quirk, especially because one was white and small, a Honda Accord, and the other was big and black, a Mercedes-Benz - opposites! But then I thought he must be just using one for his business, whatever it was - he was often away for weeks at a time, I think, though I wouldn't swear to that, or how often; and the other one, the Honda, was for local use, shopping mainly; that's what I thought, anyway.

Yes, they would both be in his garage at night, summer or winter. I guess he'd only leave a car out if he was going out again soon, something like that. So it would be unusual for him to leave one out at night, especially in the snow. And also unusual for the house to be left unlocked with all the lights on inside, when he wasn't there - as was reported in the *Spectator*. No, I didn't notice anything that night and I have no idea what might have been going on there. If the dog barked, I didn't pay any special attention; she often barked at nothing in particular, especially at night.

So - I'm no help, I'm afraid. He was a mystery man, our Mr Mc-Gregor! I hope he's alive and that you'll catch up with him, wherever he is, if only to resolve Ancaster's curiosity!

It was a pleasure, officer.

He was strange, eh? Like, childlike. Yeah, you could say innocent. Sweet-natured, eh. Bundle of energy, always dancing around. One time the wife and I got into the lift and him and another guy, the one in 1105, they were yelling and dancing around, the both of them, and the lift was bouncing around, eh? It's some joke he's told, he was always telling jokes, thought he was quite the wit, eh.

He was a smallish guy, eh? But he had quite a buff body, must have spent half his life working-out - wanted you to know it too, always wore the latest fashions, Gap is it now? Jacket and jeans, and his T-shirt, or muscle-shirt I think they call it now, was so tight you could see his tits, eh, and his jeans were so tight - well, you know, you got to

*leave a few things to the imagination, eh? "Vulgar" the wife said and
I had to agree. "What do they want to do that for? Indecent", that's
what she said. "You don't know where to look."*

*No. Nothing else. Didn't see the guy much, didn't get to know him,
eh. Into drugs maybe? Or coulda been one of them male prostitutes?
Some bad types in this building now, it's going downhill, we're looking
for a new place. Looks as if he could have gotten what he deserved,
eh.*

*Strange men? Lotta strange men in this building, eh. And the wife
says I'm strange, eh! But yeah, I did see some men in the elevator
last coupla weeks, but they could be residents, how do I know, lotta
strange men in a big apartment block like this one, these days - that's
why the wife wants us to find a new place, eh. Before anything bad
happens to us. Junkies, alcoholics, you name it, I guess they end up
with you and your guys if they don't get a knife in the back first - or
the front, wasn't it, in this guy's case, eh? There's some nasty rumours
going round.*

*Yeah, well I hope you get the guy that did it. And you have a good
day!*

She not good voman. She how you say inadekit mother? Kids
shouting running in passage I nearly knockit over one time. She not
how you say control.

Mens? Yes yes, many many mens. They knocking looking her all
time.

Five mens, maybe. All times. She not good voman.

I see man he with her he come in her place Saturday lunchtime. She
call her kids.

No more I see no more. I go out in afternoon I working I cleaning.
I come back eight nine. Police here.

She dying? Sorry, sorry. But not good voman!

Man, he was way out of his depth. Over the top. Out of his league.

*Well, I'm sitting drinking a beer, minding my own business, watch-
ing the game, you know on one of them TV screens, it's in a bar. And
this guy comes and sits on the next stool - yeah, I'm sure it was the
one, it said in the paper that he had a scar over his right eye. Yeah,
he was a small guy, well-built, and man, he could talk! Well, I wasn't
paying close attention to what he was saying at first, I was watching
the game, see. Then he buys me a beer, then I got to buy him one. Then
he leans over and whispers in my ear do I want to score some speed,*

so then I look at him, and then he says he got E, coke, crack, hash, speed, he got those five and he got access to more, whatever I want. I can come to his place and see what he got. So I say No, not interested, and he starts joking, like he never said nothing, then he finishes his drink and says See ya and goes off. And I'm thinking Man, you going to get into a heap of trouble, Mister! See, I know he doesn't know squat about how drugs is done in this burg. There's big guys out there you don't want to annoy, man - they don't have no sense of humor when they see you playing around in their territory. It's Russian roulette, man. Playing with poison. Sticking your neck right out.

Yeah, well I know people who know, that's how I know! We all got connections. I don't do drugs, like I say, and if I did would I be talking to a policeman? Not likely. I'm trying to help, man. Doing my civic duty, that's all. Play my part. Do my bit. I liked that little guy. He was harmless, I'd say, and he had that big wide smile and I always like a guy who can smile. Man, there's not much in life to smile at! And if he was doing what I think he was doing, he got to be needing money bad maybe. Live and let live, I say. And put a smile on your face! My father used to say "Misery loves company" and that's true. My mother used to say "Smile and the world smiles with you, cry and you cry alone" and that's true too. Man, I'd like a beer! Got time for one?

Well, it's been a pleasure to talk with you, Officer.

No, I didn't know the mother. I wish I *had* known her. I did think of trying to put some pressure on her to come to our parents' nights, or just come in and talk to me after the end of classes one afternoon, but she had already ignored a couple of polite notes I sent with Eric.

Oh yes, I think he would have given them to her. He was an intelligent boy with a lot of potential; in fact, with a little more support, and better attendance, I thought he could really begin to fly. But he was quite easily distracted and often seemed very tired, found it hard to concentrate some days - that's something I wanted to talk to her about. Some children are allowed to stay up too late watching television, playing video-games, and so on, nowadays. And he was away so often. She did once come to see me, but that was to complain that he was being bullied, and she got quite angry, almost abusive, when I said I hadn't seen any sign of that, and in fact two of the girls had complained that *he* had thrown snowballs at *them*. Anyway, as I say, although she said she was concerned about his work and progress, I didn't see much sign of concern. When I took the opportunity on that occasion to ask why he was away so often, she was evasive - said he would wake up sick and if she made him get up he would vomit. I wondered about his diet, whether she was giving her children proper food rather than fries and Coke. But I'll say that for her, she always came to meet Eric at 3:30 when school ended - and his little sister, Susan I think her name is - and she'd walk them home.

Oh I don't think she was a bad woman! Not at all. I hope you don't think I'm saying that. I think she was struggling. She was a single mother. Petite, about five feet tall, attractive in a way, dyed yellow hair and bright lipstick, and she tended to wear bright T-shirts with jeans or very short skirts - but then I'm old-fashioned and conservative in my tastes. Nervous manner, as if she half-expected trouble. I think she probably had quite a hard time, and I did wonder, seeing her coming day after day to meet the children, when she could quite easily have expected Eric to walk the little sister home - I don't think it was that far for them to walk, and this isn't an area where you have to be very concerned about the traffic. I mean, I wondered if she was worried about something else, say a man, ex-husband perhaps, endangering the children - well, one never knows, and I've seen some bad situations like that in my time, even at this school.

No, the boy never mentioned being concerned about a father or other man, or any violence in the family, though I don't think I ever actually asked him that directly - you have to be careful what you ask, and how and when; you don't want to cause them to worry unnecessarily, do you? And it could have angered the mother too. You do have to be careful. And he and his sister hadn't been in this school all that long; about a year at most. One of the saddest things is to see children, often children with real potential, intelligent and sensitive, being handicapped and dragged from school to school by parents, often a single mother having to move away from debts, not being able to pay her rent out of the welfare check - it's very hard to see that, and not be able to do anything about it.

Well, I'm sorry I can't help. And I can't say how sorry I am about that little boy, Eric, being hurt like that. I hope he will survive, and not with some severe disability. One can only hope that the mother too, if she survives, and the little girl, will be all right.

Yes, I am his cousin, Officer. That's right. We grew up together, more or less.

In Hamilton, yes. The North End, just five blocks apart. His Father and my Mother were, like, brother and sister, but his Father ran off with another woman when he was a small kid - and after that he had a bad time, he'd get beaten by his Mother and that man she lived with, I hated him too with his smelly breath and his fat ass, and at school he was always in trouble, had a loud mouth, real cheeky, like - the teachers hated him, he'd never do what they said, he could never sit still, jumping around in class, talking to other kids, making faces behind the teacher's back, we was in the same class once, he's two years older than me almost and they kept him back and then they expelled him.

Yeah, I guess you could say they thought he was a troublemaker, but he was lots of fun, always joking around, and he never, like, hurt anybody, he only wanted to be friends with everybody. He was, like, a clown, always clowning around, that's what one teacher said. They would laugh sometimes, the teachers, he could get them laughing with his jokes and goofing off, clowning around, always clowning around. I missed him, I didn't want to go to school any more after he was expelled, soon I dropped out. My Dad was mad when I did that, he sent me back, but I dropped out again, I hated that school, I got a job in a gas-station.

Drugs? Yeah, I was smoking weed, all the guys were. That's when me and him got together again, he was doing drugs big-time. No names, eh, Officer? You said you just want to know, like, what I can tell about his life so you can find the bastard what murdered him, you said you won't use it against me, right? And anybody else, right? But no names - only, like, what was going on. Right.

No, I don't know. You think if I had any idea I wouldn't tell you? What they did to him was - it was, like, vicious. Cruel. I know it's not official, but word gets around, and they're saying he was tortured so bad the bed was a lake of blood, they gagged him and tied him down like an animal and tortured him. And he never hurt nobody, like I said. Never. You couldn't find a gentler guy. So what they want to torture him for like that, why, why?

McGregor? Yeah, I come across him, I know who he is. Yeah, I heard that - disappeared into thin air, you can't find his car, and nobody knows where he is. No, I don't think it was McGregor who did it, I don't. Is that what you think now? I think that's crazy, honest! Not him!

Why, because he's too soft to do that - he was, like, a boss, wasn't he? Wouldn't dirty his soft white hands. I reckon he's dead, too, somewhere, with knives sticking out of his soft white back. Cement boots on his soft white feet. If he did it, he got someone else to do it, not himself, paid for them to do it. Trust me.

Well, once we was Inside together, him and me, when we was kids. We was nicked together, smoking up in a stairway, downtown, it was "contrary to probation conditions" is how they say it, eh, and we was both Inside for, like, five months. That's when him and McGregor got together first, McGregor liked him, they was always laughing, having a good time, smoking-up - McGregor always had dollars, lotta dollars, lotta influence. The other guys kept out of McGregor's way, even Harvey did, he didn't mess with McGregor. Nobody messed with Mc-Gregor. So - that's all I know about him and McGregor. McGregor did good for me too, Inside - I guess he asked him to look after me too, you need friends like that in jail, eh - but I never seen McGregor outside, don't want to. I guess he frightens me, one of those big bosses who can smile while they squash you like a worm.

No, then we was out, and I got a job, got away from drugs, got away from the guys who was into drugs, even got away from him, he was in T.O. I got a job here, then I got laid off, but I got another one and I don't want to lose it, I don't want no more jail, I don't want that life no more no more no more. But he was back Inside. I heard that. He called me once, couple weeks ago, a month maybe, said he was back in Hamilton, had a good place, didn't say where, said to give my Dad his best, happy Christmas, and my Mom but I don't know where she is, she left Hamilton last year, said she was going up North. He said he would call me and we'd get together.

No, he never did.

SIX

A Child This Day Is Born

May the words of my lips and the thoughts of all our hearts be always acceptable to Thee, our Lord and Creator.

My dear friends in Christ:
Our Lord was a baby. He was *a baby*. God came to us as *a baby*.

Let us think about that for a while, this Christmas Eve, during these final hours on a snowy winter night, before our midnight strikes and we rejoice in the birth of our Saviour Jesus Christ. Christmas Eve 2000: two thousand years after His birth! And here, now, we remember, we celebrate, the coming birth of our Lord as millions have before us - His birth, His eternal rebirth, as the new Millennium of His everlasting reign awaits us.

Think of the enormity of it, the strangeness of it! Two thousand years ago, our God, the all-powerful everlasting Creator of the entire universe, Who could have entered it in any form. But He wished – our God came to us as a tiny helpless *child*. A baby. Our God chose to come to us as a baby! Let us think about the implications of that wondrous, that amazing, that startling, that *incredible* fact. God chose to become a human-being, one of us - that is startling enough. But He came not as a mature human-being, a man or a woman. He came as a child.

Why? Why did He do that? Why did He choose to lie helpless at His mother's breast, to grow up surrounded by other children, to obey

- once, even, at least, we know, to *disobey* - his all-too-human earthly parents? Of course we dare not assume that we can ever know God's reasons, but we can guess, my friends, humbly we can guess, with the aid of Holy Scripture. We can guess that He chose to experience to the full all the stages of human life to adulthood, to experience frustration and pain, yes and fulfilment, joy, like us - just like each one of us. He wished to experience *as a human-being* the life of human-beings, the daily life that *we* live - fully to experience it, in all its complexity and confusion. To understand *us* - I do not think it is blasphemous to say this - so that we can understand *Him*.

Did he experience the challenge and excitement of sex? I remember wondering that when I was training for the ministry, so long ago now - I asked one of my teachers, and he changed the subject - but that was before our liberated days, of course, even before the publication of *Honest to God*, and that dates me! - before one was permitted to ask such questions! But I believe He did - He must have, it stands to reason he must have, if He became a human-being like you, like me. He must have wrestled with sexual desire, struggled to control his impulses just as you do, as I do. But He prevailed over those desires, He controlled them as we so often fail to do - He had the spiritual strength to remain pure.

But I digress - those of you who know me know how prone I am to digress! But I hope for your tolerant forgiveness. And especially as this is my final sermon in this church where I have loved to serve my God and all of you, my beloved friends in Christ. Some of you, and especially if you are not a regular member of our parish family, will not know that I am about to go on leave, and will not be returning as Rector of this parish. I will say more about that later. At this point I merely wish you all to know that what I say now will be my final formal words as your priest. But I am in God's hands, as we all are. He will decide the future of His servants. But let me return to my main point - if I can recall what it was - I can see that some of you are wondering if it is lost for ever!

But no. Yes. He did not come as an adult. God came to His earth as a child, a baby! Do we understand this, I wonder - do we even attempt to think about it deeply, all that that choice of God's implies? For me, it is one of the most important, perhaps even the crucial, fact of His coming into the world. The Nativity - that's what the Church calls it. Oh, we're all familiar with the term, aren't we? But let us think for a little while, together here in this beautiful warm welcoming holy building, God's building, while the snow falls and cold winds blow outside, and some other human-beings created in God's image, some other human-beings not far from here, are *not* warm and protected and well-fed and contented and looking forward to celebrating Christmas joyfully with their families tomorrow as we are - let us think, as midnight approaches and we prepare for the miracle of God's nativity, let us think about the meaning of that stupendous decision, that divine choice. I say it yet again: *God came as a baby.*

What do you see when you imagine the Nativity? So many of our images of Christmas, so many paintings through the ages, so many of our favourite Christmas carols and hymns, focus on the Holy Mother and Child. "To you this night is born a child Of Mary, chosen mother mild; This tender child of lowly birth Shall be the joy of all the earth." "Silent night! Holy night! All is calm, all is bright Round yon virgin mother and child. Holy infant so tender and mild, Sleep in heavenly peace, sleep in heavenly peace." Oh, I could go on and on, and you could too - And our deeply loved Huron carol: listen to the words closely when we sing it later in this service. And the first hymn we sang tonight - we sang it with a will, we bellowed it, didn't we, because we all love it, know it in our very bones, don't we? - "While Shepherds Watched Their Flocks By Night". Let me repeat some of the words we sang:"The heavenly babe you there shall find To human view displayed, All meanly wrapped in swathing bands, And in a manger laid." "The heavenly babe" - lying there helpless, prickled by straw, breathed on by sheep and oxen - then lifted to His mother's tender breast for sustenance, while His earthly father Joseph looks on protectively.

Ah, Joseph! Joseph. Do we see him too, as we imagine the Nativity scene? Well, if the evidence of centuries of Nativity representations, in painting, in sculpture, in all the arts, is accurate - no, Joseph is often just not there. Do you see him? If you do, he is standing in the background, perhaps in the shadows. Joseph the husband of Mary and the foster-father of God. Why should he and his role be so neglected by us? Of course, he *is* a Saint - but as I have often said to you, so are we all! And the Church, in medieval times and later, has formally celebrated his sanctity, and he is the patron of a good death - which of course we all hope for! But it does seem to me that to associate him with death does not do justice to Joseph, who was in his life associated with *life* - with new life of a baby, with the eternal Life that is God, and that Christ's coming offers to all His creation.

Joseph! This is what I see when I look at him, standing strong and protective beside his wife and the baby Jesus. I see a lovable kindhearted generous man, a model for every man in an age when men are so often and so automatically excoriated as selfish violent brutes! Do we even think of what he did for us, I wonder, and the tests he faced and so triumphantly surmounted? A baby not his own - he was laughed at, sneered at, no doubt, as a cuckold, or a liar; and a young wife still a virgin, yet pregnant before they have even slept together. A long dangerous journey, with no money for they are poor - it is easy for us to underestimate the dangers and discomforts, the diseases around them, on that journey! And their destination, or rather where they found refuge for Mary to give birth - we are inclined to sentimentalise that stable, aren't we? It probably stank, it was probably filthy - how could it not have been? - it was a hovel for animals. And certainly you and I would not wish to risk the health of our baby, or even of ourselves, by breathing that air, touching that straw! And now Joseph's young wife is groaning in the final stages of her pregnancy - in this hovel, fit only for keeping animals, no doubt smelly and dirty, as I said, no place for a wife giving birth, let alone for the new-born child. But he perseveres, he is there protecting them, he finds food for her, he brings water, he uses all his strength, all his determination, in his love for his frail young wife and his bastard child - yes, bastard child in the eyes of his society! Are you shocked that I say that? "Conceived out of wedlock"! Christ was conceived out of wedlock. But his earthly father protected Him, gave Him all the love and protection He needed to survive and then grow into His maturity.

And after the Nativity, Joseph's role as protective father does not end - maybe it becomes even more difficult and dangerous. You know the story: Matthew and Luke tell it. According to Jewish tradition, the child Jesus, as first-born, should be presented to God in the Temple; so another journey to be undertaken, to Jerusalem this time - accommodation found there - and it was there that another man I love, the old Simeon, lifts up the child and rejoices. And yet another journey, the most dengerous of all, when Joseph is warned about Herod's coming holocaust; not for a moment does he hesitate - and he is leaving so much behind him, and uprooting his family - it would have been so easy to wait and see, to find excuses - but "he arose, he took the young child and his mother by night, and departed into Egypt". 'Departed into Egypt': another deceptively simple statement, but think of the work, the effort, the danger they faced. And then surely it was a struggle to survive, to find work, to find accommodation. And when he is told to return to their homeland, again he does not hesitate, although there is extreme danger in Judea so that they must go to Galilee, another place unknown to them, and finally settle and make a new life in Nazareth.

Just think of all that disruption in their family life.

We think of Joseph as a carpenter, since the now-mature Jesus is identified as "the carpenter's son". But that might have been how he had to earn his living - who knows how much his life changed during the years when he gave up so much to support and protect his wife and fos- ter son. There is a tradition, too, that he was an old man when he mar- ried Mary. If that is so, isn't it all the more admirable that he gave up so much, worked so energetically, protecting and sustaining his family in harsh and often-dangerous situations? But in truth we know little about Joseph as a person. Each one of us is mysterious, impenetrable; we do not know well even our closest friends and family-members - or ourselves. Remember that after I have gone: you are a mystery: and I do not, I cannot, know you in any but superficial ways - and I am a mystery to you. In that respect, Joseph is emblematic. He is Everyman - or rather, what every man can be if he has the faith, courage, and love that we see in all that Joseph did. He did not seek to judge and con- demn others, he did his best in very difficult circumstances, he acted positively, to save, to preserve, to protect what would otherwise have been hurt or destroyed. It is what Joseph *did* that is important; that he offers us a model of how the good husband and the good father should behave, what his values should be, and how they should be put into action. *Action*! That is what I love in Joseph too: he is a man of action, a pragmatist who does not allow his doubts and reservations to get in the way of what must be done.

After Joseph's roles and responsibilities, as father and husband, have been fulfilled - after Jesus has matured into a confident young itinerant preacher, taking God's message to all who will listen - Joseph simply disappears from the Gospels. His job is done - well and tru- ly done. Now the story is about Jesus. What happened to Joseph in his later years? Did he die before Jesus was crucified? Otherwise we might expect him to be standing again beside his wife, his arm round her shoulders, yearning to protect the foster-son who is suffering and dying on the cross. But it doesn't matter - he can do no more. What he has done was infinitely important, and he did it well. That is all we need to know.

I love Joseph! Every one of us should love and admire Joseph! And especially men should love and admire him, for he is the model of what every man can and should be. He is a model of the good husband and the good father. I don't know about *you* - the men who are still, howev- er bored you are right now, however unwillingly you are still listening to me - but I know that *I* have not been the good father and the good husband that I could have been. I have failed in protecting my wife and child, I have failed in courage and generosity, I have failed to love them enough. I have come close to despair. And then I needed Joseph. I need his example. I need him to help me pick myself up and try to be the man *he* was. God needed Joseph's love and protection, and Joseph was up to the task - he was a true man, a true Christian. And God needs you, He needs me, just as we need Him.

So. In this rambling Christmas sermon I have taken you on a journey, several journeys. But all the journeys are leading us to the same destination, which is God. And when I get there - *if* I get there - I hope to meet Joseph and hear the rest of his story, the part that is not told by Matthew and Luke - and I bet you a loonie to a dime that he is a damn good storyteller too! In this sermon, if that is not too dignified a word for my disorganized thoughts and hesitant words, we journeyed from the baby Jesus in his Mother's arms to the man whose job it was to protect them, sustain them, in partnership with God to ensure that He survived, and grew from baby to child to boy to man - and finally carried His cross to Gethsemane. But that is another story. Though it is also all one story.

So I must say goodbye, not in sadness but rejoicing in God's mercy, rejoicing in the many years we have journeyed together in God's service. My journey, my story, moves now in another direction. I shall be literally and metaphorically travelling in other lands for a time. I rejoice too that the parish will be in the good hands of the priest and dear friend who will soon stand beside me to offer to you all the body and blood of the risen Christ - Who is born tonight - so soon, so soon - and will die on the cross, and live forever, forever, forever.

Praise be to God. Amen.

And now unto the Father, Son and the Holy Ghost be all glory, now and forever more. May God have mercy on us, may His love enfold us and give us peace. Amen.

SEVEN
Truth to Justice

1   Monday 14 January 2001
      Mysterious Disappearance of Ancaster Resident

Local newsboy Brett Holliday (15) raised the alarm on Sunday morning, when he arrived at the upscale residence of Daniel McGregor, and discovered the front door open and lights on.

"I immediately suspected something was wrong," Holliday said. "Mr McGregor is a very organized guy. There was snow piling up in the entrance hall. I shouted for him but I just knew somehow he wasn't in there. So I called the police on his telephone."

Holliday explained that he did not usually visit McGregor on a Sunday morning, but he had found a telephone message from him when he awoke that morning.

"Mr McGregor sometimes called and invited me in for coffee and to talk for a while on Sunday mornings," Holliday said. "I deliver his newspapers during the week, and after a while he said how he would like to talk to me sometimes, about music and computers and stuff.

"He was always waiting for me, early every morning, when I delivered the papers. I guess he didn't sleep too well. My Mom said he must be lonely. He wasn't married or anything. He lived on his own.

"Some guys said he must be weird, and to be careful, and my Dad said that too, but he was always friendly to me and he would give me $10 if I went on Sunday mornings."

McGregor is well-known to the police, and has twice spent time in prison. He is suspected of being a "drug-lord", and is thought to have many criminal contacts in Ontario and beyond. He is also suspected of possible involvement in two unsolved local murders.

When he was last arrested and in custody for drug offences, the charges were eventually dropped, after one of the two main witnesses was killed in a car accident, and the other withdrew his evidence, claiming that he had made it under police pressure. At that time McGregor threatened to sue the police for wrongful arrest.

The police believe that he may now be on the run, however. The larger of his two cars, a black Mercedes-Benz, is also missing, and it is possible that he crossed the border into the United States in it on Saturday night, and could have left the United States by now, as he is known to have contacts in South America. Interpol and police in North and South America are actively searching for Daniel McGregor, who has no known relatives.. Anyone with information is requested to contact their local police station.

2   Monday 14 January 2001
      Man sought for attempted murder
      Wife and son attacked with hockey-stick

A nation-wide police alert has been issued for Derek Simpson (29), who is regarded as dangerous, and described as of medium height, slim, with very short fair hair and a scar above his right eyebrow.

He is suspected of having fled a scene of violence on Saturday night, leaving two bloodied family members on the living-room floor of their apartment in West Hamilton, and another screaming in terror.

Those screams caused neighbours in the apartment building to run to the family's aid, but they could not gain admittance to the apartment until the police arrived and broke down the door.

Samantha Simpson (3) is now temporarily in the care of one of the family's neighbours, Mrs Arlene Dawe, who said: "She is doing as well as can be expected, but she cries a lot for her mother and brother whenever she is awake. She and her brother were very close."

Her mother Nancy (27), and her brother Eric (11), are in Intensive Care in the University Medical Centre. Both were severely hurt when the suspect attacked them with the boy's hockey-stick. Neighbours speculate that the boy had attempted to intervene between his mother and the suspect, who, they said, was not his actual father.

The suspect had recently been released from prison. He has a lengthy record of convictions and imprisonment, both for drugs offences and assault. Two years ago, he was sentenced to two years in prison for domestic assault.

One neighbour, who did not wish to be identified, said the mother had mentioned that her husband would be returning soon, and that he was an alcoholic who became violent when drunk. The mother had admitted that her husband had beaten her and her son before, and she had been forced to seek protection in a shelter, but she also said she still loved him.

He had assured her that he was now cured of his alcoholism and was taking appropriate medication, including Antabuse pills, so that there was no chance he would ever be drunk and violent again. However, the neighbour said she thought the woman was fearful, because of what had happened in the past.

McMaster Medical Centre would not comment on the present condition of the mother and son, but Mrs Dawe, who had been present when the police broke down the apartment door, said it was obvious that the mother had been very severely wounded.

"There was a lot of blood. The boy, Eric, didn't seem so badly hurt. He was moving and crying. I hope the mother will survive. The children need her."

So far, the suspect, Derek Simpson, has not been apprehended, and he may have left the Hamilton area. Anyone coming across him is advised to exercise great caution, and is requested to inform the police immediately.

3   Tuesday 15 January 2001

MARTIN, Margaret Jane - Passed away peacefully at McMaster University Medical Centre, on Friday, January 11th, 2001, on her seventieth birthday. Beloved wife of the late Rodney A. Martin. Loving mother of Jonathon and Elizabeth. A Graveside Service will be held at Eastlawn Cemetery (Section 21) on Tuesday, January 16, 2001 at 3 p.m. In lieu of flowers, donations to the Heart and Stroke Foundation.

4   Thursday 17 January 2001
Horrific Murder Stuns Hamilton
First in 2001: 'Bad Start to Millennium'

The body of a murdered man was discovered in his penthouse apartment yesterday morning.

He is John Smith (26), who has also been known recently as Brad

Scott or Tiger Martin.

He has been living in Hamilton for four months, after being released from Maplehurst Correctional Centre, where he had been serving a fifteen-month sentence for selling cocaine and other drugs. He had a lengthy criminal record, beginning in his teens.

In Hamilton, police state, he had become involved in the sex trade, but may also have been trafficking in drugs again. The expensive rental of the penthouse suite in which he was living may indicate that he was part of some well-financed drug ring.

It is thought that Smith was murdered some days ago, probably on Saturday night. Detective Inspector Cuthbert Fogarty said: "Forensics will determine more accurately the exact time of death, but present indications are that it was some time during the night of Saturday January 10th."

The discovery was made by a visitor, who telephoned the police yesterday morning but refused to identify himself. He said he rang the bell of the apartment several times but there was no response. "He also said he noticed a sickening smell," Fogarty said. "And yes, there was a lot of blood in there, as we found when we entered the apartment."

The police will give few details of what they found, but they do concede that Hamilton's first homicide of 2001 was an especially unpleasant one. "All murders are unpleasant," Inspector Fogarty said, "but yes, you could call this one 'grisly'. It was grisly for sure. This is a very bad start for the Millennium."

There is some suggestion that the victim had been tortured, and that the murder was in "gangland-style". However, Inspector Fogarty said: "That is all speculation. It is early days yet. We have a great deal to find out before we can solve this case, but we will solve it for sure. It is imperative that the public be protected from horrendous crimes of this nature.

"We will not allow Hamilton to become Murder City. The murderer of John Smith cannot sleep secure, whoever he is. He will be found and tried for his heinous crime. Justice will prevail."

5   Friday 18 January
Naked Corpse on Ski-trail is Wanted Man's

When Jane Gimley (24) slipped off the ski-trail yesterday afternoon, trying to avoid what seemed to be a log on its edge, she did not know she was about to solve a murder that had occurred five days earlier, 250 kilometres south, in Hamilton.

Still showing signs of shock as she sipped hot chocolate in her parents' home in Owen Sound, she said: "I fell right over sideways, into soft snow thank the Lord, and when I got back up and was re-attaching my skis, I could see that what I had thought was a log might be a body, so I scraped away some more snow and suddenly I could see a face.

"Then I had another shock. Because I knew that I had seen that face just recently!

"Just a couple of days earlier, when I was last along that trail, I came across this young guy walking along the trail in the other direction.

"I always feel irritated when walkers do that, because they can muss up the trail for skiers, and that's who it's made for! So I was about to say something about that to this guy, but I didn't. He looked sort of, like, sad, lost - I don't know how to say it - almost like a little boy lost, and his clothes looked too big for him. I just felt sorry for him.

"We talked for a few minutes, I can't recall what about, nothing special. But I do recall his eyes and thinking how beautiful they were - they were very blue, intensely blue - and that he was kind of handsome, attractive. You know, cute. I was thinking 'I wouldn't mind getting to know you' - the way you do when you meet someone unexpectedly like that.

"But then I had to go - it was getting late, and I didn't want my parents to be worrying about me. They hate me going off skiing on my own! But there's nothing I like better than that - snow and silence, and you just glide through it forever - it's the greatest feeling in the whole world!

"But I don't usually ski the same trail again straightaway - there are so many great trails up here - so now I wonder if I didn't go back there because of him, somehow. And then it was so scary to find it *was* him! Right there, lying right there under the snow. And he was dead!

"His eyes were closed, thank the Lord. And of course his whole body was completely frozen.

"And now they tell me he was a wife-beater and alcoholic and a murderer and all that. So maybe I had a lucky escape. That's what my parents are saying."

The naked corpse that Jane Gimley fell over was in fact that of twenty-nine-year-old Derek Simpson, wanted in Hamilton for assault at the time he fled the scene of his crime last Saturday night, and then somehow reached the Bruce Peninsula in the middle of this very severe winter!

The police speculate that he was given a lift by an unsuspecting permanent resident of the area, and then broke into a summer cottage not far from where his corpse was discovered. They are appealing for information from anyone who may have seen Simpson or given him a lift last weekend.

A charge of murder was added to the assault charges against Simpson last Monday, when eleven-year-old Eric Harper died after two days in Intensive Care. His mother Nancy, who was attacked at the same time as her son, is said by friends to be out of danger now, and likely to survive.

Now that Derek Simpson's corpse has been discovered, at least the taxpayers of Ontario will not again have to bear the financial burden of paying for the trial and incarceration of a monster.

But Jane Gimley says there is one trail on the Bruce Peninsula that she will never ski again!

6   7 October 2003
        Ex-Priest found Not Guilty
        Judge advocates 'reconciliation'

Paul Preston (66) walked out of a Hamilton courtroom yesterday a free man, after being found not guilty of sexual harassment. After being charged with that crime two years ago, he immediately resigned from his position as a minister in the Anglican Church.

Preston spoke briefly to reporters on the steps of the courthouse before leaving with an unidentified woman friend.

"It is a relief, of course," he said. "I have lost so much, obviously, since the accusations were made - but, God be praised for His goodness and mercy, I have been given so much too.

"I have learned how destructive Satan can be when he manages to enter and pervert human hearts and minds, and convinces them that they have suffered great evils that must be avenged.

"As I said from the beginning, I am innocent of the charges that have dominated my life. I tried to help and befriend those teenagers - as they were then - not to harm them in any way.

"I am grateful to those who believed me, and have given me their support - I can never thank them enough. At times, I confess, I came close to despair, and to losing my faith in God and in human goodness.

"I do not blame those who accused me, and those who say, and may still say, that they think I was guilty. I forgive them, as Our Lord forgives us all. I pray for them, and for us all, that we may learn to love each other better and, with God's help and wisdom, find it in our hearts to understand each other better, and to forgive each other. "That is all I have to say at this time."

As he was walking away, Preston suddenly turned, walked back to the assembled media and said, with a smile: "I am beginning a new life, you know, but it is also the old one. God is making me into a new man, but I am also an old one, as you see! Remember: when you have nothing, you will find that you have everything. God bless you all."

Preston, who became known as the "Pedophile Priest" while on trial for sexually molesting the six complainants at a summer camp in the Dundas Valley some thirty years ago, resigned as Rector of his church at the end of 2000, soon after the first complaints against him were received by the police and communicated to him.

Known then as Father Paul, he had been a priest for thirty-seven years, and was deeply loved and admired by his congregation, who were stunned by the nation-wide controversy following his arrest and the widely-publicized charges against him.

His wife left him at that time, and testified at the first trial that the evidence given by the two initial complainants supported a suspicion that Preston had sexually abused his own daughter, who was disabled and has since died.

The two complainants were teenagers when the offences were said to have occurred, at the summer camp where Preston, then in his early thirties and unmarried, was acting chaplain.

When that case was dismissed in August 2002, after the two complainants admitted that they had colluded in fabricating some of their evidence, four other women came forward with similar accusations. All six accused Preston of sexual interference and harassment including inappropriate touching.

While insisting on his innocence, Preston admitted freely that he remembered hugging and even kissing several young people at the camp. "I thought they needed love and approval so badly," he said. "They were deeply unhappy, and obviously glad and grateful when I listened to them."

All six complainants agreed, under cross-examination, that they had indeed been unhappy at the time. Two of them admitted that they came from "dysfunctional families", and all said they had been emotionally distant from, or in conflict with, their parents.

They testified that they had "bonded" at the camp, had kept in close touch with each other subsequently, meeting twice a year for dinner and a show, and had come to understand that Preston's behavior towards them was primarily responsible for various problems that had developed in their lives, such as sexual dysfunction and marital break-down.

Justice Mary Gwynn, at the conclusion of what is her final case be-fore retirement, addressed the jury after it found Preston Not Guilty yesterday, owing to a degree of reasonable doubt.

She said: "This has been a difficult and highly controversial case but I think that you have come to the right decision. It seems that Paul Preston behaved naively and very unwisely many years ago, and that he has paid a very high price for that.

"Yet he has impressed me as being honest, to the point of damaging his own defence, and as a man who, in the eyes of the angry, judg-mental and sceptical society in which we live today, perhaps took his vocation as a priest too seriously - especially Christ's injunction that we should love others as we love ourselves.

"I think that Preston loved 'not wisely but too well'. But he *did* love, and I wonder if our society needs more people who will love as he did - more wisely, yes, but also as well as he did.

"I hope that this case, and all its implications, will be considered deeply by our society. But I fear that is unlikely to happen: in two days' time, it will already be yesterday's headlines, and we will hurtle on-wards, imposing our often-hurtful judgements on others, not out of knowledge and careful thought, but in conformity with what some call 'political correctness' - or, worse, in conformity with our own selfish hopes, desires and delusions.

"I am glad that we did not behave like that here today. But I know what has been suffered, deeply suffered, by all those involved in this case. The six complainants may now feel - but I hope they will not - deprived by our system of justice of that 'closure' they sought; and Paul Preston has endured years of public vilification, the loss of his priest-hood, the loss of his wife and daughter.

"It may not be enough - indeed, I know that it is not enough - but I offer all of the principals in this case my best wishes for happiness, fulfilment, reconciliation and peace in their future lives. I hope you will not allow remembered pain to imprison your spirits. I hope you will find peace."

7   September 2015
        "Triumphant Triptych"
        An Interview with Marvin Mercier

We found our now-internationally-famous artist with a glass of

water in one hand, the other being held by his lovely daughter Samantha, who is now almost as well-known as her father - she is the superb
young prize-winning cellist for whom Tamara Beckstein recently composed her stunning "World's View Concerto."

Our artist was clearly uncomfortable in a somewhat close-fitting
suit, but his so-solicitous daughter was smilingly radiant in a charming
gown that matched the intense blue of her eyes!

We persuaded our artist to grant us a brief interview, before the
public opening of this his latest and most eagerly-awaited show. We
spoke to him mainly about the show's center-piece, the towering work
that all of Ottawa (and the international artistic community) are waiting to view.

Us: Marvin, you must be pleased and excited about this show, and
all the buzz about your "Triumphant Triptych" that has preceded it -
your first religious paintings since the great "Stations of the Cross" and
"Seven Gifts of the Holy Ghost"?

Him: Yes, I am, I am! Of course, those two series are, and must always remain, in the two churches for which they were commissioned.
But it means that most people know them only as small-scale repro-
ductions. But this "Triptych", here in the National Gallery, will be seen
as it actually *is* by all who want to see it - and no doubt by many who
don't!

Us: Can you say briefly what this work is intended to communicate
to us?

Him: Joy. In one word: joy. (He laughs loudly.) The joy of creating,
the joy of creation, the joy of God's Creation. Like Molly Bloom, it
says Yes, Yes, Yes! To life, to humanity, to God. Look at the colors, look
at the soaring structures! That's why I call it "Triumphant Triptych".
Everything hums, everything glows, everything soars. You see, the earlier two religious works were focussed on the suffering of Christ at the
Crucifixion, highly realistic in expression and content, although many
of the critics found that series symbolic; and then the mystical "Gifts",
with each one - Wisdom, Understanding, and so on - represented
by collocations of symbolic color and structure - well, you have seen
them, I assume. (His hand sweeps upwards, cascading water.) I have
completed the set of three *with* a set of three; all interlocking, utterly
complementary - internally as well as externally - you see what I mean?

Us: If you say so! (Sometimes we are rude to painters whose work
we admire!)

Him: I was fortunate with "Stations of the Cross". It just came, it
was. As you will know, it realistically transcribed aspects of my prison

experience and observations, fifteen years ago. I simply thought about suffering - Christ's suffering, my own suffering, the suffering I had caused, and of course the suffering all round me in prison - and I just *painted*. It came. Perhaps because I was so innocent - about art, I mean! I had to work harder, much harder, on "Gifts", and I was much less satisfied with it - which is partly why, for so many years, and in spite of requests and offered commissions, even this one by the National Gallery, I turned away from religious themes. But that turned out to be a good thing, because I developed new eyes, new hands, new styles - I needed to, so I could express all those other ideas that came thrusting into my brain - the "Death of Green" series, for instance. Then, last year, I know - Well, certain events -

Us: (Finding a space in the flow!) "Certain events ...".?

Him: Events in my personal life that I would rather not talk about. You know how I try to keep my personal and artistic lives separate.

Us: Yes, but you paint so deeply out of your personal experience - you have often said that yourself! You have just said it again! So, is it fair to refuse to talk about it?

Him: An artist must protect his deepest sources from pollution - even by himself!

Us: But surely you can comment briefly on the names that appear so prominently in the three glorious paintings before us. (Hey, we can do compliments when we need to!).

Him: All right, then I will. Sam, could you find me some more water? (His daughter goes off to fulfil his request.) Now I'll get out of my Alter Ego's hearing and whisper a few highly personal statements for your readers. Which they may not be able to understand. - No, don't print that. (So we just did!) Look at the middle painting. The most prominent name is Nancy - I probably don't have to tell you that that is my wife's name. And yes, I can see you want to ask why she is not here tonight. But Sam's here in her place - here she comes with the necessary libation, just before my throat seizes up. Thank you, my darling. (He swallows some water.) You can also see Sam's name if you follow the flaming yellow spiral upwards - see it? And a third, the name of the Catholic sister who arranged the commission that made me paint "The Stations". My three blessed women, my saints, my inspiration. The feminine, the female, that is the centre of all things. See how they dance together, my three blessed women, raising their arms towards God. See how it all pulsates, the whole pattern - in the fecundity of color, the joy of life, all surging, surging, surging up towards God!

Us: Yes. (Uncertainly!) And the names on the other two paintings?

Him: Yes. Notice that the colors are darker generally, and how they writhe against each other, in competition not cooperation now, egotistic, demanding, color against color - angrily, destructively, on the left; calmly, constructively on the right - pushing downwards and outwards in the left painting, inwards and upwards in the right one. The male principle competing, seeking to assert, to organize and control, wrestling with demons inside and out. Separated from the female but yearning towards it, towards life, creation - always prone to wrench and destroy. But there is ultimate reconciliation, in creativity, in God, as the great overarching pattern completes itself triumphantly in the "Triptych" as a unity, the two male patterns linking, fusing, with the female. There are two names in each of those two paintings. Four altogether. Those names are Derek and Tiger on the left, Brian and Eric on the right. All four, the males who have given me their lives and their love in spite of themselves. Do I know what I am saying any longer? How will I cope when those doors open in a few minutes and the lions roar in to devour me? Sam - more water? Thank you.

Us: You said that the four men are all dead?

Him: Dead? Yes - dead, and alive. Eternally alive. Derek, Tiger, Eric long ago, aeons ago - and yesterday, today, tomorrow. And now Brian. Gone too. - No, I can't say any more. (He seems to be weeping. His daughter puts her arm round his waist as he turns away from us.) Brian. He died a few weeks ago. He took his own life - his wife and their two sons were killed earlier in an accident near his wife's family's summer-cottage at Port Hope, one of the sons was driving - and he - Brian - he wasn't in the accident but I guess he couldn't face living without them - I didn't know anything about it, nothing at all, till a letter arrived - you see, I hadn't seen him for four or five years, lost touch with him after I started going overseas, shows, art-galleries, you know - but he wrote it, this letter to me, the night before he - Said he was going away, a long journey - I called his law-firm, he was a well-known litigation lawyer, Brian Harrison, he has a very high reputation as you surely know, he won a famous case, you'll remember it, fighting insurance companies over responsibilities to clients - But his office, and our mutual friend Peter Abbott, said they didn't know where he was, he had left instructions that nobody was to look for him, that he was going on "the longest journey", that's what they told me. And you see, his death completed a pattern: all the women are alive, you see, and all four men are dead. So then I knew I had to complete the Triptych, and found I could, so I did. And one other thing I must say to your readers: four men, three women. You see? My Seven. But also the universal, the eternal, the joyful seven. *Your* Seven. Union of substance and spirit through art. Through God, who is art. Who is everything and nothing. The Word. Do you understand any of this? Do I? I don't think so! And I won't remember a word of it tomorrow myself, probably. Now I must go and put myself together again before the doors open. (He rushes off as we try to thank him. So we thank Samantha instead. She smiles graciously, and perhaps anxiously, as she takes up a post near the Men's Room.)

So, readers, we offer you the words of an artist who has written "My advice to any artist is: Shut up! When they ask you to explain what you have painted - shut up! When they ask you why you painted it, why you paint at all - shut up! Shut up, shut up - and paint, paint, paint!" Well, who said artists are any more consistent than us lesser mortals? They may be divinities, but they are also mortals! And our beloved Michael Mercier is a very mortal divinity! We love both the man and his art! What say you?

8   10 January 2021
What happened to Daniel McGregor?
One of Canada's greatest unsolved mysteries

It is now almost exactly twenty years since Daniel McGregor, a middle-aged man known to the police for his criminal activities, disappeared from his palatial home in Ancaster, Ontario.

The police file on his case remains open, and some important information has been added to it over the years, but the likelihood of its ever being closed seems to have receded greatly. Some would say that the case will never be solved now - unless McGregor himself suddenly reappears, or a body is discovered and proved to be his.

A police spokesperson stated, when I made enquiries about the present situation: "It is not true that there has been inaction or complicity on the part of the various police forces, including Interpol, whatever may have been said in the media. Very considerable time, effort and money have been expended, in Canada and around the world, in the ongoing attempt to locate Mr McGregor."

The spokesperson also pointed out that, because the solution of several other cases would seem to depend on locating Mr McGregor, the police have every motivation to continue the search, and are in fact under continuing public pressure to do so.

"We want badly to talk to Mr McGregor," the spokesperson said. "Until we we have definite proof he is dead, the search will continue. Any information that might help us will be very welcome."

The case is not, of course, unique. A similar case of disappearance - that of Mafia "Kingpin" Rocco Perri - is often cited as a parallel. Both men were known to be involved in high-level criminal activities.

One Hamilton police officer told me: "You know what they say? If we could dredge every corner of Hamilton Harbour, we'd find quite gathering of skeletons wearing cement boots."

But the McGregor disappearance is notoriously mysterious and elusive. Very little definite information about his activities has surfaced, and few of those who might be expected to have knowledge of them have been willing to talk. Why?

The man himself is mysterious. Remembered as quiet and calm, with piercing light-blue eyes, a pale complexion, soft voice, very large soft white hands, and a flabby body, he seems to have aroused immediate respect, and even fear, in all who knew him.

We know now that he was involved in some of the worst unsolved crimes at the turn of the century in Southern Ontario - especially in Hamilton and Ancaster.

Since his disappearance, on the night of Saturday January 14th, during a heavy snowfall, the murders of a prosecutor and a lawyer who had in the past opposed him in court, and of two petty criminals who had signified willingness to testify about his drug-dealing activities, have been very reliably linked to him through the testimony in court of several members of the underworld.

Other suspicious deaths, and many beatings, have also been linked to him. However, there is disagreement about whether, and in what way, he was connected to major crime syndicates, like the Mafia and Hell's Angels. Some claim he was a member of both.

However, it is his undoubted involvement in two Hamilton crimes on the same day in January 2001 that has recently aroused renewed interest and speculation.

The first crime was the horrific torture and murder of John Smith (24). Recently released from prison, Smith had a record as a pimp, male prostitute and drug-peddler in Toronto.

No-one has ever been charged for this crime. However, new evidence, largely in statements made by the notorious Hell's Angels boss Bart Harvey, under questioning during his recent trial, indicates that Smith had fallen under the influence of McGregor while in prison. When murdered, he was living in an expensive penthouse apartment in downtown Hamilton which, police believe, was financed by McGregor.

The second crime was an assault on a woman and her eleven-year-old son (who later died in hospital) in West Hamilton. The suspected assailant was her husband, a violent alcoholic, Derek Simpson (29) - who, according to Harvey, had also formed a close relationship in prison with McGregor. Simpson was found a few days later, dead, on a ski-trail on the Bruce Peninsula, 250 kilometers north of Hamilton.

By then it was known that McGregor had disappeared. As had his black Mercedes-Benz.

Now the story becomes confusing and complex - worthy of a detective novel, perhaps, if only the plot could be unravelled!

It was at first assumed by the police that there was no connection between the two crimes. They surmised that McGregor - responsible for or connected in some way with the murder of Smith, for some motive yet unknown, but probably connected with the drugs-trade - had fled to the United States in his Mercedes-Benz.

A watch was put on the border, and police everywhere in North America (and ultimately everywhere in the world) were alerted. But the car was invisible - until, four months later, it was found in a garage, on the Bruce Peninsula, not far from where Simpson's body was found, by an astonished cottage-owner (who had just returned from wintering in Florida)

This fact opened a whole new range of speculation. Simpson's fingerprints were found, among other evidence, on and in the car. Did he steal the car from McGregor's residence, and flee north in it? Had McGregor already disappeared by then? Or did he drive McGregor north, then - perhaps after a quarrel - murder him and dispose of the body before dying himself? Alternately, did McGregor murder Simpson by marching him naked to his death at the point of a gun?

Yet other possibilities have been suggested, linking the two crimes even more closely. If Smith was murdered for a purely personal reason (rather than one connected with drugs and prostitution), could that indicate that Simpson was responsible for killing Smith, either on his own or under McGregor's orders?

There is support for this theory in Harvey's testimony. He claimed that McGregor had a homosexual relationship in prison with Simpson that was destroyed by the arrival of Smith, who replaced Simpson in McGregor's affections.

A further link between the two crimes came to light in September 2015 when Nancy Mercier, wife of the well-known artist Marvin

Mercier, but married to Simpson when, it was claimed, he attacked her and killed her son Eric in January 2001, told the police, shortly before she died of cancer, a fact that she had denied earlier but now wished to confess, presumably to square her conscience.

This fact had been suspected by police, after neighbors of the Simpsons claimed that they had seen Nancy Simpson entering or leaving a vehicle that, their descriptions suggested, may have been McGregor's Mercedes-Benz.

Nancy Simpson-Mercier now confessed, just before she died, that she had had a secret relationship with McGregor, having learnt about him from her husband, and that she had been running drugs for him, to make money to pay for her cocaine habit (which, she said, she had managed to kick after the disaster of her son's death). She claimed that Derek Simpson, already drunk, became enraged when he discovered this, and attacked her.

But where does this plethora of information leave us? Your guess is as good as mine!

So what *is* my guess?

That Derek Simpson, who was a vicious brute, murdered Smith, and then attempted to kill his own wife, in both cases to avenge the loss of his close homosexual and drug-running relationship with McGregor, and that he then attacked, overpowered and, after driving him north through the winter night, murdered McGregor, before committing suicide.

A colleague of mine believes that I am right off the map. He believes that Simpson was not responsible for any of the violence, even for the attack on his wife and her son. The only witness of that incident (the son, Eric, died without being able to answer questions, and the three-year-old daughter - now the admired cellist Samantha Mercier - was in bed and did not witness the attack) was Nancy Simpson. Why should we believe her? She had good reason to lie – and, as we now know, did lie..

My colleague surmises that McGregor, whom he describes as a monster worse than Evelyn Dick or Paul Bernardo, committed both crimes, possibly forcing Simpson to participate: that he murdered Smith, then attacked the Simpson mother and son (perhaps because she had deceived him), and, after he had forced Simpson to drive him north and was no longer useful, he murdered the latter - and took on a new identity! Well - that doesn't convince *me*!

But what is *your* guess? Send it in, preferably by e-mail. The most convincing guess will win $100, and the best four will be published in the next four Saturday editions of this newspaper.

So get your brains humming! My colleague and I both believe that one of your guesses may give us the truth.

However, unless Daniel McGregor is found alive, will we ever know that it *is* the truth!

EIGHT
Hanging Rough

1

March 1st 2002

Dear Old Buddy!

You always hated that I called you Old Buddy, didnt you? Maybe thats why I did it! Old Buddy! Just to rile you up, in the old days, at high school, remember? Guess I was jealous! In fact - yeah, I *know* I was jealous! You were always so smart - top of the class, good-looking too - and the girls all gaping at you, competing for you, yearning for you, trying to climb into your pants! They didnt look in my direction at all! Even tho I was so hot - I would have given them a real good time, in bed and out of bed, so I reckon it was there loss!! You were so good at sports, football as well as hockey (I wasnt bad, but you were *good*, I got to admit it - "He aims, he shoots, he *scores!*" You could have been the next Gretzky, the next Great One, if you wanted - thats what I thought! (I bet your two little guys are good too - those hockey genes and you to teach them!) Also you could write poetry too (puke!), and sing like Gordon Lightfoot (double-puke!!), and play the guitar (triple-puke!!!), and all the teachers were just so honored to have you in their class. You were the Hero, you were "The One Most Likely to Succeed" in the Yearbook. Remember? And you did succeed, Old Buddy! The rest of us sat and drank in the bars and played pool and smoked weed and cigarettes and got fat and lazy - you were right to move on! (Last time you visited, said you thought you were a failure!! - I couldnt believe it and I dont! Marriage problems, your boys getting bad marks,

69

and how you dissapointed your parents, how you failed your first year at Mac, partying, boozing - but then you picked yourself up, did good at Mohawk College, I forget all you said - done some bad things I didnt know about!! - but you didnt hurt anyone or get your name into the newspapers, did you? My freind, look at it like this, *Im* hanging rough but *you* hanging *in* there!! - you done so much, paid your way, good citizen and a real good guy, my freind!!!) Oh, and I forgot about your brillant acting - remember when you were King Arthur in *Camelot* and all the girls fighting to be Gunevere? You looked so good up there on the stage that even I fell in love with you! (Hey, maybe thats when I became a pedophile, what you think??? So, all your fault, Buddy!! - So, yes, guess you are *evil*!!)

So why am I writing all this Garbage, Brian? Out of affection and admiration, better beleive it! I mean it!! You are way better than any of us knew! You a failure, a bad guy? You are truely a *great* guy, Brian, Old Buddy?? I truely mean it. At school you were the only one I truely admired, deep down, only one I really wanted to have as my freind - but you hardly noticed me, there were so many others wanting a peice of you, teachers, other guys, and all those girls. But its a funny old world - Now you are my freind, all these years later! When I really need you, Old Buddy!

This will be my last letter before I come out, my dear freind. The last one! In nine days, I will sign all those papers and get my clothes back, and the guards (sorry, "correctional officers"!) will shake my hand and look me in the eye and wish me good luck (hoping all the time that Ill be back soon, Im their bread and butter!! but dont count on it, I wont be back, hey, Bernie and Pete and Willard and Randy, I wont be), and theyll unlock the door and out Ill walk and the sun will be shining and the fresh air of Ontario (!) will blow through my hair and you will be there! And Ill shout "Freedom, freedom, freedom!" Thank you for that, too, my freind - I know you are very busy up there on the Mountain in your garage and I apreciate that you will be there waiting for me, and drive me back to Hamilton.

Yes, you are a true freind, Brian. None of the others, all my old drinking buddies and such, none of them came through for me, they all turned their backs, even my closest freinds (or I thought they were!) like Steve and Brett, they were ashamed after the first time, to think that anyone might remember that they ever even knew me - a pedophile, a pedophile! A Child Molester! Who wants to be connected with a Child Molester! And his name is in all the newspapers, on TV, "a danger to children". (I hope they dont do that again. Do you think they will? Then everybody just hates you, they just want to chase you away somewhere else, anywhere else, you have no home!) But you came through for me, Brian, and Ill never forget it. You even offered to help me get a job in your uncle's garage - I cried after that, my friend. I hope you understood why I said no - not because I think I can do better, Ill do much worse (who wants to employ an ex con - a pedophile ex con! but Ill get some job nobody else wants, in a hospital maybe, cleaning up vomit and shit!) I said no because I know what would happen with the other guys in the garage - theyd all pack up and look for new jobs! Suddenly nobody to sell your new models! And nobody to buy your new models!! (Brian bankrupt! Your wife would murder me!!) So I hope you know I truely appreciated the offer, Brian - I did! But Ill be all right, Ill find something! (I think I *have* something! - see below) I want to stand on my own two feet! Besides, thanks to you also, I have a family to go to. Yes, you are a true freind, Brian.

So Now Im hanging rough! Did I ever tell you what that means? Its prison lingo for the last few days before you get out. You get antsy, you cant wait but you got to wait, so thats the time you can hit the wall, do something wild. And the other guys are envious, they thinking about Outside too, girlfriends, wives, kids, all that - and they give you lots of free advice, and they hit you on the back, and its freindly but its also angry - somtimes they hit you so hard you wonder if you got to put your fists up, but you look at them and they smiling too - hurting inside but smiling outside. So its a hard time when you hanging rough! You just want the time to go fast, to be out, out, out! So you rite crazy letters like this! My crazy letter to my Old Buddy Brian. You dont even need to read it if you dont want to! Its my Hanging Rough Letter!!! - the only one youll ever get!

So Ill write every day till the day I see you. That's the plan. Help to keep occupied, keep me out of mischief! Also today is 1st of the month, March - funny, I decided to start this letter before I saw that, so it must be meant by God! He is with me, He is with all of us. He is the One! So goodnight - sleep well. Talk to you tomorrow.

2

So Here I am again. Im sitting in my cell writing - chewing the pencil! I told Gary to shut up so I can think (hes my cell mate, young guy, twenty-one, in for shooting his girlfriend - fortunatly his aim was off that day!). (Just kidding. Sorry, Im trying to stop joking like that, I know its bad - its the old me, the old bad Marv, just habit.) Now what else do I want to write, my friend?

(I had to go and play cards with some of the guys for a while.)

Oh, I almost forgot to say Thanks for coming to see me, and accepting those calls, we had some good conversations! - and for writing me - in Millhaven and Warkworth - thats a long way for you, other side of Toronto, but you visited eight times! And now one final time soon! Nine visits! I remember how it was, visiting at Barton Street Jail, how you qeued up in the cold - I did it when I was out, more than two years ago it was, and guy I knew was inside, I promised his girlfriend tht Id visit, she had to go home to New Brunswick, her father was dying - and youd be standing in that long qeue hearing the life-story of the guy behind you, or a young girl in a flimsy dress is smoking and coghing in front of you with her baby, taking it to see its Dad (I dont approve of that!) - and how slow the qeue moves, and you just hope they would get on with it, so when you finally get to the entrance itll be "Next!" through the intercom, not "No more visits today". And then you wait on your steel seat, and finaly here he comes, like a clown in his orange jumpsute!! You look at each other thro the plexiglass, and all along its two people looking at each other and then talking thro those phones, and you sound just so far away - and you *are* so far away, even tho its only two feet! And the others talking away on both sides, so loud sometimes you cant concentrate on what you trying to say! And you dont say things you realy want to or about important things, you talk about the weather and such! Not like realy communicating, like being together and realy talking, but its all you got. And hey it realy matters!!!

You dont know how much those visits ment for me, my dear friend - when you came that first time, I was so surprized when they told me who it was! (You said you just passing by, on the way to pick up yr wife from yr inlaws farm, but still it took time and effort!) How much I looked forward to yr visits after that - just seeing yr face smiling on the other side of the plexiglass, talking through the phone and even tho we could hardly hear each other - but it made me feel I mattered to someone - wasnt just dirt!!! You havent been in here, you havent done what I did, so you dont know how much it meant for me, my freind. So thank you for that too!!! (It gave me some self respect, hey.) Oh yes, and for the money you put in for my canteen. Ill pay you back, all of that money, I promise! Youll see - soons I earn some, Ill start paying you back. I know you said not to worry, you dont need it, you not poor and its a plesure - you a real generous guy, I know that - but I want to pay it back, and I will, for me, not just for you! (I kept a note abt how much.)

I know I can say all these things when I get out and we can talk proply and have a coffee together. (You dont know how much I long to go into a Tim Hortons and have a coffee with you! I shouldnt even think about that in here, specially while Im hanging rough!!! I could go mad and bash my brains out!) I know I can tell you everything then, and I will, but I want to write it down now, before I get out and before I am with you - just to be sure, and so you know I realy do mean what I say! And sometimes its harder to say things but you can write them? (And I know I got a reputation as a joker! Dont even know if Im joking sometimes, my dear freind, its a habit from feeling so inferor to you at school hey! But none of THIS here is joking. I AM GRATEFUL, TRUELY!!!) So goodbye for now. Ill post these pages tomorrow.

3

More Hanging Rough letter! 3rd of March - the time is going, slowly, slowly. But I think

(Had to stop. There was a lock down - think I told you about that, they do it quit often - makes you go back into your cell and the guards go round searching for drugs. Sometimes you got to strip and bend down and they look up your ass!) Then after lock up ended I had to play cards for a while. Dont want to annoy the guys, especially now! And I think helps them to feel happier too, that you still with them, still one of them, and you wont forget them whn you outside. Funny how at first, both times after I was inside, I felt frightened - that all the other guys hated me, that they were waiting for an oportunity to kill me, but then you find out about them too - everyone tells there story here, everyone gets to know, and you better not lie because if they find out you lied, then you in trouble! You find that some of them done worse than you, maybe, and you get to know them as individuals, and you get to like some of them and avoid some and to tolrate others, there problems, long as they dont cause too much trouble, because you are all in it together, just like being in the army, in the war, I guess - us and them - comrades, sort of, depending on each other, working together against the enemy! You dont get to be freinds, real freinds, because always some danger, guys who can sudenly hurt you if you let your gard down, but you get to be comrades, you get used to each other, living together in this way - no women, no kids, no routine, no responsbilities, just do what you told and look after yourself and make sure you dont cause problems for your comrades - and do things with the guys like playing poker, dont lie and cheat, dont swear at a guard and dont snitch and dont ever look in another guys cell and dont ever *ever* whistle - and then you all right. The Inmates Code, what they call it! I know people outside think theres a lot of violent sex, big guys raping smaller guys, like in the movies, but thats all garbage I think - if anyone was to be raped, youd think it would be me!! (Maybe its because Im bigger and fatter than most of them! - and not very sexy to look at now! Or maybe its true what the guys say, that they put stuff in the water here to try to make you impotent, but I think its mainly because theres no stimulation, no women, no variety, no challenge, just boredom, montony, here inside.)

So thats what its like inside, my freind! Can be almst a pleasnt existence - if you dont think about what you missing thats outside! If you want to avoid all problems, have peace like a corps in a grave. If you dont want a real life! I can understand how easy to becom what they call "institutionalized"! (Hope Im not! Dont think so - looking forwrd too much to my new life outside!)

Did I tell you about what Jesus means to me now? I know you dont believe in God, you said you were, what is it - an agnostic? I even feel a bit embarassed to tell you about this - I was always the joker, always laughing at any of the guys who had anything to do with religion. (Remember I made poor Ralphs life a misery - Im ashamed of that, wonder what happened to him? I hope he has forgiven me, or forgottn me.) Ill tell you about it later, how I found Christ - no, how He found me - through a little old lady volunteer, Rhoda, at Barton Street, she did a program in cooking! (I know how to make brownies now!) and Grace here and also the Chaplain - but no time now, soon be lights out. Also about my paintings, Ill tell you about them too - thats connected with religion. Everything is connected, praise the Lord! Th whole universe, all of us, you, me - all one Unity! Praise the Lord.

Goodnight, my frieid. Ill post these three days to you tomorrow - this letter getting so long! Youll go blind if you read it all! (If you *can* read it all!!)

4

Writng all that about life in here ("My Life in Prison" by One of Society's Evil Outcasts!) - I hope it didnt bore you!!! But made me think about Tiger. Remember how I called you and asked you to buy those Tina Turner tickets way back, over a year ago, wasnt it? First time we spoke, I phoned you at your garage. (Im so glad I did that, now, tho I felt so embarassed and humilated when I did it - in fact I nearly *didnt* do it.) The tickets were for him. It was when he came here to Warkworth, from Millhaven, second time we was together - but he was differnt this time, I guess we all change, he didnt joke around so much, and we didnt do our Laurel and Hardy comic routine no more (I dont think we could have done it here anyways) - and he kept more to himself (but I was happy with that because I was working hard at my "Stations of the Cross" paintings by then, that was all I wanted to do, couldnt think of nothing else all day and all night, my mind was just ful of wild ideas and shapes!), but sometimes we would talk together still, Tiger and me, and then later when he was hanging rough and thinking about when hes out, he said to me if only he could get a ticket to see Tina Turner he would be extatic, he would be so happy he wouldnt mind dying, and then I thought of how he helped me when I was afraid and I thought of you too (and I hadnt thought of you for a long time, better believe it!!) because I remembered we always liked her, you and me, and how we joked about her, that was one time you seemed to notice me! - and then just when Im calling you he asks me to ask you to buy *four* tickets! - so thats how it happened, my freind!

His real name wasnt Tiger, by the way, that was a nickname, and then he called himself Brad after he got out, one of the guys said - but after he was murdered they put his real name in the paper? Anyways, he was a real friend to me when I needed one, just like you, Brian. When I was first in Barton Street, before my first trial, two years ago. Thats when I met Derek too. And Tiger was a great guy, we got on just fine, joking around - he was smart like you, and full of life, full of fun. (One old guy in there called us Laurel and Hardy, remember them? - I was Hardy, the big fat one, and Tiger was skinny little Laurel - he was a small guy, Tiger, but good looking, slim but he worked out a lot, even got me working out once or twice!) If youd ever met him youd like him, everybody liked him - no one would dare to harm him, even the boss guys. We would both crack jokes, Tiger and me, but he was funnier than me, real witty sometimes, and then he would crack us all up! We also did a sort of comic routene together, Tiger and me, just happened to do it one day (you know the sort of thing - "Hey hey hey, what's your name, Mister?" "Nothing." "No, you can't be Nothing, *I'm* Nothing! So what's your name?" "Nobody." "No, you can't be Nobody, I saw Nobody all yesterday!") And so on. Stupid stuff, but the guys found it entertaining - even some of the guards did - theyd beg us to do it every few days, but of course we had to keep it quiet, keep the noise level down in case anyone got the idea we were starting a prison riot! So I thought Tiger was a really good guy - kind, genrous, and brave too. In here you get to know what a guys made of. I remember how bad I was afraid, the first few days inside there, in Barton Street - pissing myself, I have to admit that. Even tho it was 3A, the Psychiatric range they called it, where they put guys with bad problems, like sever drug addiction, or anxiety disorder, who need a lot of medication, and also guys they think might need protective custody, I thought Id be stabbed to death - you know, because of being gay - and the one I thought was the big boss there, Harvey (theres always a big boss, or some guy who thinks he needs to be one) - he sent a message he was going to get me. But Tiger comes to me and puts his arm round me and says out loud "Hey, Old Buddy, come and join the game, you can play my hand, I got to take a leak" and after that I had no trouble. Harvey, and his lot left me alone after that. Or perhaps it was just Harveys little joke, that - saying hes going to get me, to get some fun for himself and the others, out of watching me piss myself - you never know, you just have to watch your back and hope. I wonderd what Tiger wanted from me, at first - he was gay, anyone could see that, in fact he drew attention to it! - but then I saw he was already set up with a quiet older guy, McGregor. Those two were cell mates, they would spend a lot of time just talking quietly to each other on the range.

Then I got to know Derek - he was *my* cell mate, and he was respected there too. But he didnt like Tiger. Before Tiger came, McGregor was very friendly with Derek - he told me that, and he said Tiger bad mouthed him to McGregor, but he and McGregor still were freindly - they had a "special understanding", Derek said, and they would talk together if Tiger wasnt around, or if Tiger and me were joking around, doing our Laurel and Hardy for the guys. McGregor hardly ever talked to anyone else, just sometimes he just sort of smiled at me - his eyes were pale blue and he gave me the willies somehow, but when Derek was shipped off, to OCI I think, and then Tiger too - he got a tough sentence, McGregor started to talk to me sometimes, called me over - said hed like to help me when I get out, any freind of Dereks and Tigers was a freind of his, and I should contact him when I get out - but I never realy trusted him somehow. (I dont know why - he just made me feel creepy, with his deep, soft voice and his bald head and his little smile and those pale blue eyes looking deep into your eyes but sort of vacant.) I could see that the other guys, even Harvey, were frightened of him - they kept out of his way. Then he was out, his lawyer got him out, they dropped all the charges, for assault - attempted murder I think. I remember some guys said one of the witnesses was found dead, another one changed his story and gave him an alibi. One of the guys here says hes a big "drug-lord" with lots of influence, even in the Government, and I saw in the paper the other day (one of the guards brings in the *National Post*) that the police are saying he was a "criminal kingpin", suspected of having Mob connections. I dont know. They still looking for him, arnt they - all round the world?

And the police say they still have no idea who killed Tiger? I been thinkng about that, who might have killed him - I realy liked Tiger, like I said, and he was a good freind to me, a gentle man who wouldnt hurt anyone. They say - the guys here - that he was tortured before he was stabed in the heart. They say he was found naked, tied to his bed, and the bed was just a lake of his blood. Thats what upsets me - not just because of the pain he would suffer - nobody should die like that, especialy a guy like Tiger who did nobody no harm. Makes me feel sick just to think about it. Poor guy if thats what happened. Poor Tiger.

So who do I think killed him? I think McGregor, maybe - not jst him, he would have had some younger guy to help him and do the dirty work while he watching, I think. (What do you think?) Should I tell the police? But they wouldnt believe me, and it could be trouble. And whats happened to McGregor? Where is he? Some of the guys think hes dead too, now. They think the Mob is involved - like the guys say the Mob killed that lawyer and her husband, up at Ancaster, was it? Or a biker gang - Hells Angels, Harveys big in Hells Angels and they say he hated McGregor and any guy McGregor liked. So maybe Harvey and his biker guys did it. And one of the guys here, Lennie, he says a friend of his who was inside with Tiger at the Don was HIV-positive, and he says Tiger gave it to him - and he swore he would kill Tiger, realy make him suffer, before he died himself - and he died of AIDS about same time Tiger was killed. But why am I writing all this? Its nearly lights out, I got to stop soon.

Also maybe I shouldnt be writing this stuff, they censor our letters - but you always say nobody except you can read my writng anyways!!! And this letter is extra badly written, isnt it? These little stumps of pencil they give you to write with, "golf pencils" they call them - my fingers start to ache after a while, and the pencil slips in your fingers too! Maybe you won't be able to read any of this (its getting so long anyway!) But Ill read it all to you when Im out if you like! So goodnight! Old Buddy.

I'll post 3 and 4 now. This letter getting too LONG!!!

5

I been thinking - you see so much suffering in here, but you cant talk about it! All the guys are suffering - and trying not to let any of the other guys know what they are going through. Why do we do that, when we could help each other? I guess we're all frightened of showing our weakness, and the boss guys most of all - if they show any weakness, theyll lose there power and there position. But why is it weakness to tell the truth? Isnt that the opposite - telling the truth - isnt that being *strong*? But nobody believes that in here. So you just have to keep your mouth shut, even when you longing to talk about your feelings - the pain you are in, deep inside. Thats why we need Jesus.

6

Are you still trying to read this, my freind??? My writing so hard to read, I know that, specially with this small pencil, but I think I been depressing you too, with all that stuff about pain and suffering. Sorry! I hear you saying "Lighten up, Marv! Whats hapened to you? You were always the life of the party, joking around" and I was, I know I was. But look where it has got me!!! (I woke up depressed this morning, you can see!) Well, I will make an effort to get on top of myself now!!! (Better than being underneath myself!)

First, I got a lot to live for! Second, I got friends (like you), and great support. Third, Jesus will help me - I have given my life into His care, and the Chaplain here says He will never fail anyone who truly believes in Him. Truly, I should put Him First! Brian, I didnt write about this to you before, because I thought you might laugh at me. Remember how I always made fun of religion before - at school, and when we played hockey and went drinking?

Sorry, I dont feel too much like writing today, dont know why.

7

And good morning! Another day of Hanging Rough, but it's getting close now - 7th March today! Its hard not to look and act excited! I long to see you, my friend. And I long to be with Nancy and Sam! I hope youll drive me to there place! I know you will. But well have coffee first, in the nearest Tim Hortons? Then youll drive me there.

Look, you dont think I know, my freind, and yes I was trying to pretend that I dont know - Nancy asked me to keep it a secret and please dont blame her becaus I cant keep it any longer! I want to thank you for that, too, my freind. You never told me! Nancy said you just arrived one day - she said you told her you had read about her and Sam and what had happened, in the paper ?) - and how you wanted to help, and give them some money to pay for the rent and such, and she said no, no, she coud manage, and anyways why did you want to so much - and after a while, she says, you told her you know me, and how I told you how much I loved them and was so sorry about what happened, never wanted to hurt any of them, just trying to help with looking after the two kids while she was away visiting her friend in Guelph, and so sorry about Eric, the poor little guy - I still miss him, know that? - and about him being killed by Derek, and how I blamed myself for that too, because Derek was my friend and also I gave Eric the hockey stick he was killed with - all of that. But you know it all. I was so surprised when she wrote me (it was a long letter, and a Christmas card), and I replied and sent her and Sam a card, and we went on writing, almost every day, long letters, some almost as long as this one!!! and then she sent her number and said I could call, and we had some long talks - and she let me talk with Sam too (she said Sam wanted to, cause she remembered me and said I was "that funny kind man who told stories and played games"!!!).

I said please would she forgive me if she ever could. She said "Nothing to forgive" - that she knows now that Eric was right - what he said at the trial, that I was his freind and I never hurt him and never would hurt him - and thats the truth, Brian, its the truth! How often I ask and ask what was going through my mind - and the psychiatrists ask me too - because of the first time too, when those two boys said I touched them, and I did, but I didnt hurt them, I never wanted to do that. But I dont know why I touched them, except I think maybe they reminded me how I was so happy when I was their age. (I can't explain it any other ways. But I know it was sexual too, Im not trying to pretend it wasn't.)

I suffered a lot, Brian, trying to understand what is inside me - what made me do those things with boys - and psychiatrists too, asking me all those questions, talking, talking - and I still don't know for sure, and that worries me too. I know I must never do it again - I'd rather die than do it again! But how can I be sure that I wont? Only make sure I can never be with little boys again, maybe. And I think God will help me too. But I hope you will help me too, my freind, the way you have helped me all the time I been in jail this time.

Goodnight! Sweet dreams!

And you know, after that first time, when I came out after two years, there was that huge publicity in Hamilton (do you remember that?) - my name in the *Spectator*, warning to the community, all those people screaming at me, wanting me to be sent away somewhere else, letters in the paper, reporters waiting for me - but I had a Circle of Support, people who made a group to help me and also try to make sure I wont re offend, and they helped me. We would meet, like freinds, and talk and pray together, and they would ask me how things were going, and do things for me, and give advice, and call me to talk about things, and meet and have coffee with me. I feel so ashamed that I let them down. I told them that. They gave me so much time and love. You see, I should hve told them about getting to know Nancy and her children. I knew it was wrong to deceive them, but Derek had told Nancy about me, after I got to know him in jail, and he made me promise to go and see her and tell her how much he was wanting to be with her again. So I thought the Circle of Support would have to tell the police if they knew, and then the police would stop me going and spending time with her and the children - and when I got to know the children I just loved so much being with them. (My mother always said she was just a child at heart, so perhaps I take after her!) The worst thing I did was to say I wuod look after the children, give them a holiday on Sams birthday, so Nancy could visit her friend in Guelph, and then I took them to that cara-van-park. The owner was a family friend - we used to go there every summer, my parents and myself, when I was little, and my parents got to know the owner very well. And I rembered how I had my ninth birthday there and how it was the happiest day of my life - it was just a few days before my father died. So I wanted Sam's birthday ther be really happy too, a day she will always remember - and I guess she will, but not for being happy, not the way I wanted it. But I was wrong to do that - it was against my probation order and I knew that. (I guess I sort of hoped to get away with it, and told myself it was worth the risk.) They said in the trial I had "groomed" the children and Nancy, but that wasnt right. Anyway, three of the members of the Circle of Support say they will carry on and be my next Circle, so I will be in good hands - theres, and yours, and Nancys and Sams, and Ill have to report every day at first to a Parole Officer.

It was Nancy who suggested that I can live with them, and she per-saded all the others to agree. She said she would take responsibility for me! You know how we have talked about it so much. I know I have to be careful, especially as I dont understand what goes on in me - why I am attracted to little boys, and I dont want to risk hurting any kids. The medication will help, they said, but Nancy doesnt beleive in the medication - she says that if I am happy with her and Sam, I wont even be tempted to re offend. She says that Ill be alright with two females in the house - theyll keep me in order! I told her I dont know about sex with her (just to be totaly honest), and she says she knows, and shes had enough sex to last for rest of her life!!! Well see what happens, she says. She wanted to know all about my life, and she thinks I am attracted to boys because of my fathers sudden death - it was a heart attack, and after that my mother would hardly let me out of her sight, she was so frightened something might happen to me - she was a very loving woman, but also she smothered me, Nancy says, and so I stoped being able to be, like, a little boy, do the things boys did, and she turned me into a girl, sort of, so thats why I became so intrested in boys. Then she died of cancer when I was 18, and I went to live with my grandmother - Maybe Nancys right, but whether she is or not, its going to be different with me this time! I know my luck!!! With them, and you, and the Circle of Support, I will make it! I beleive that, Im confident of that now.

And if you hadnt visited Nancy and helped her, it wouldnt be happening, Old Buddy! She wouldnt of writen to me. Yes, I know about the other guy, the divorced one who lived in the same building and then he went back to his wife! A black guy, a real gentleman, she says - hes a prof at McMaster, in Engineering I think. He asked her to marry him, and she said yes, but then his wife wanted him back, and threatened to go back to Trinidad with his kid, if he didnt go back to her, so he did - how can you blame him, she says. He told her he didnt love his wife, and he loved Nancy, but he couldnt face being seprated from his son. She told me all about that. I don't mind. He was a good man and Im proud he loved Nancy - Ill try to live up to what Nancy told me about him - his kindness and sympathy and support. I think it was Gods doing, I think it was God giving me a break! Praise the Lord! I couldnt be happier about it. I love her and Sam and they love me. We will live together in Gods love. Praise the Lord!

And theres her two brothers too, Mike and Stan. Mike called her after Eric died, when she was still in hospital, and then he came to see her a few months ago, and he paid for Nancy and Sam to go and have a holiday with him and his wife - they dont have any children, and they just loved Sam, Nancy says - and they want to meet me too. (Mikes wife heard about my paintings - she's an artist.) And Stan - had a bad time and when he comes out next year, Nancy wants us to help him. I know him a bit - he was also a freind of Dereks, inside, and he was my cell mate for three weeks in Barton Street after Derek, quiet sad guy, he was in for assault that time, not drugs - his girlfriend had left him and gone off to the States with an American guy she met, and taken their kid. Nancy said she was hard and mean, that she had just used Stan all along and then taunted him and accused him of assaulting her so she could get rid of him, and they werent married so he has no rights as the kids father, Nancy says. So she says she wants us to help him when he comes out.

Enough words for one day. I guess you agree!!! Nearly lights out, anyway!

8

Sorry, I cant write anything today, just a few words. But one thing I got to tell you - I know you a lawyer! So now - But I like to rember you when we talkd about Tina Turner that first time, remember?And you say youll buy those tickets for me and you did!You spent money, you trusted me!!!! You were a true freind and Ill never forget, Brian. Am I crazy??? No, I dont think so.

Only one more day to go! I don't think thats why Im nervous, I just dont know why. Everything seemed dark, as if the sun was gone for ever. Grey, dark, like the end of the world.

One reason was, I dreamed last night about Eric and I woke up sweating and shaking. He was smiling at me but he was blind, like they said in the paper, and blood was running out of both his eyes, he was lying there and the hockey-stick was lying next to him, the hockey-stick I gave him for his birthday, the one Derek hit him with. If I hadnt given him that hockey-stick, if Id been ther not in jail, if he had never known me, if I hadnt been Dereks friend - if, if, if!!! I woke up and I was moaning over and over "Forgive me, please forgive me" and he was smiling, just smiling, but the blood was running down his face.

I stayed away from Graces program this afternoon, I was feeling so bad. I couldnt face nobody. But one of the guards came after it was over and said she wanted to see me to say goodbye, so I had to go. (Did I tell you she is a Catholic nun really, but she doesn't dress like they used to when we were young, just an ordinary dress with a cross on her necklace, and she doesnt want you to call her Sister! But the Chaplain is a Protestant, so Im a real mixture now - a mongrel Christian!) Anyway, when the guard took me to her, in the interview-room, she just said "Marvin, I want you to stand here and pray with me". And we stood in silence for a while, then she spoke to God and asked Him to bless me and guide me and protect me, and she thanked Him for the time we were together, and I began crying, Brian - couldnt help myself, I was shaking and crying like a child who has been hurt, and she just put her arm round me - shes just a tiny little woman, Grace, so her arm was only halfway up my back - and you know what she said? She said "Marvin, Eric loves you, he loves you and he always will love you." How could she know? How could she do that? Only because God asked her to, I truly believe that. Praise the Lord. Then we said goodbye.

Before that I was just thinking and thinking about all that suffering and death, and wanting to bash my brains out on the wall, and asking God how He could ever allow it all to happen, so much of it everywhere in the world, all the time, so many people in pain - and I was thinking so much about Eric, and Tiger, and Derek, I could see them, I could feel them in the cell with me, their gosts, and I could feel their suffering. But after Grace went, I felt different, as if I was healed from being sick, as if the sun was shining again. "The light shines in the darkness, and the darkness does not overcome it." Praise the Lord.

9

12 March 2002

So this is IT!!! My last day inside! Tomorrow morning Ill see you waiting for me as I come out the door into the sunshine, and then well have a coffee and a talk - but not a long talk, Brian, not tomorrow - I want to be with Nancy and Sam, and I know youll take me there - I told them we would be at her place at 12 and she said shed be cooking a special meal for the three of us, a celebration (she said she invited you - Im glad she did that, but you said you would need to get back to the office, after being away all morning) - so then Ill be with my family, my new family - and it will be a new begining! Praise the Lord.

I said I would tell you about my painting, Brian, my art. Im an art- ist!!! You said you would like to know all about it last time you came to see me and it is a big thing for me - Nancy says I must bild on what I done so far, she thinks I can earn money with it and even become a great artist! Well see. Maybe, with Gods help, I will be able to do that. Id like to be able to use the talent I have to make the world a better place - help people to see God, how He is there in all of us, if we will look, and especially if we will *listen* to each other, and how He wants us to love each other, help and serve each other, not hurt each other.

I think I told you I started because of a program in art in Barton Street - a volunteer, Mark, came in every Tuesday afternoon for couple hours, in the rec room. He would sketch portraits of us in pencil that we could keep (they were good, too, he did one of me, Im going to give it to Nancy). And we would sketch each other, too. Thats when he said he thoght I had real talent and I should take art lessons when I get out and see how far I can go. And he liked my other sketches, and my water colors, all my memories of places and people - he said I had a very good sense of color and design too. At school, I was good at art, too - remember? Maybe you dont - the guys used to make fun of my paintings, so I stopped trying. (You were one of those who made fun,

Brian - remember? But I forgive you, my freind!!!) Anyway, when I came to Warkworth I decided to realy make an effort - lots of time, and I could get water-colours and oils, and everything I needed, so - And then, I started some big paintings, after Grace asked to see some of my work - she had heard about my painting, and then she said she would comission me to paint a series of paintings for her church - "The Stations of the Cross" - but a modern version, she said, *my* version, for *today*, what I saw in my imagination, not another lot of Jesus carrying the cross and so on (she showed photos of some, in a book) -"Just use your imagination, and think if Christ was here right now" she said. So I did. I painted twelve - fourteen the usual number, but I thought they should end with Jesus death on the cross, the end of His earthly journey, the final suffering that ends His suffering forever, the moment when His life as a man ends and His life in Heaven begins. Like the moment I will be at tomorrow morning, when my life here ends and my new life begins! (I just thought of that!) Praise the Lord for all His blessings!

What I didnt expect was what happened after I finished painting "The Stations of the Cross". Grace took them to her church - I finished them just in time for Good Friday - and they framed them and they were set up all around the church. (Grace says she would be very happy to take me round the church to see them there, and Nancy wants to see them, so hows about we all go there on an expedition in a little while?) Grace wanted the church to pay me, put money in my account - "I said it was a commission," she says, "so you must make an honest woman of me!" but I said no - not only because all the paints and the canvasses were paid for by the taxpayers of Canada (!), but also because it was a privilige and a joy, and a turning-point, I think. Look at what happened! Someone in the congregation got in touch with a big Toronto critic, and he went to see them and then wrote an article in the *Globe and Mail*, and there was a small one in *Macleans*, and the *National Post* sent a reporter to interview me and now the *Weekend Magazine* is publishing a special article illustrated with photos of all twelve paintings, and I had letters from artists and priests and professors! So you see, if all those people think I have talent, then maybe I have! And then I must use it, I *must* - you know the parable of the talents, the Chaplain used that a lot in his sermons, saying God gives us all talents and its our duty to find out what they are and then use them.

So, Brian, who would have thought that so much good and so much oportunity could come out of my evil? That doesnt mean I can forget about the bad - I will always rember that - but I thank God for the good

He has given me. I know I will have to be careful, and always try to avoid temptation, and obey the Parole rules exactly, and work hard, but with the support of freinds, especially you, my very dear freind Brian (aka Old Buddy! - sorry!), and with the love of Nancy and Sam, and Erics prayers in Heaven, Gods will *will* be done - and His will is love, and out of the love will come truth, and justice, and unity. I believe that, my freind, and I think you do too (even if you dont know it yet!), or you would not of done all you have done for me! *Thank you.*

One last thing I must write, and then this long long long letter will end (I promise!!!). Last night, when I was feeling so depressed and everything looked grey, I was also thinking about Derek and Tiger and McGregor - and me. How the four of us hapened to meet in Barton Street that time, two years or so ago, just happened to be there at the same time and get connected, and I thought about all the bad things that came out of that, the suffering and death. Eric and Tiger and Derek and maybe McGregor too. All because of chance? (I dont think so.) If we had not met, would any of the evil, the suffering and violence and death, have hapened? Derek and McGregor were friends, and Tiger and McGregor, and Derek and me, and Tiger and me. The four of us, all linked together. And now they gone and theres only me. Sometimes I think God saved me to live for Eric - in Erics place, now that he is in Heaven. That it must be part of Gods plan, I think sometimes - otherwise why did He allow Eric to be killed like that, and why did He arrange for you and Nancy and Sam and all those others to help me and raise me up? But I also think sometimes (but I cant understand this at all! - the thought just comes into my mind) that I must live for Derek and Tiger and McGregor too, that God brought us four together for some reason, and part of the reason is so that I can live for them too - the way they could be living there lives - so that good can come out of evil, which is what God always wants. I dont understand what Im saying, my freind, my dear freind Brian, but maybe I will one day! How can humans ever understand Gods ways?

Praise the Lord.

I will give this last part of my letter to you tomorrow, and if you cant read it, all these words words words I been scribblng for nine days, you better ask me soon, becaus I cant hardly read my own writing (surprised?) and when I forget what I have written, in a little while, it will all just be meaningless marks for us both!!! And perhaps thats what they should be? You could just crumple up all these pages and throw them in a garbage can? What do words matter? Perhaps they should die, all these words, the way we will all die in a few years and be raised into the full glory of God. Gods will be done, always.

Good night. Sleep well. I know that I will sleep well tonight. God bless you.

Praise the Lord. Praise the Lord. Praise the Lord.

Your friend Marvin

NINE
Visions and Revisions

Friday 19 January - Wednesday 31 January 2001

REPORT FOR MADAM MY NEW THERAPIST

Prefatory Note (21 January): In the spirit of your challenging me to attempt "utter honesty" in this report, I state here that I will have revised this document progressively, adding & subtracting material, & finally organizing the text into ten sections. It is not, then, the imme- diate, unmediated rendition of my experiences, thoughts & emotions that you would perhaps have preferred; but it is all the more ME (or, all the more correctly, I), the apostle of order & precision. I have com- posed this document on my (primitive but still functional) word-pro- cessor (I greatly approve of this machine & its promotion of recon- sideration & emendation: as the poet put it, of "a hundred visions & revisions before the taking of toast & tea" (quoted from memory, but I think correctly)). I will also have relied occasionally on my notebook &, to a lesser degree, since my time & energy are limited, on some minor research, to try to ensure a "truthful" account of actuality. Any failures are unintentional! How regrettable it is that life itself does not (except too infrequently; all too infrequently!) permit "visions & revi- sions", so that we could live it more productively!

1 INTRODUCTION: THE QUEST

Madam my Therapist: When you requested this account of my life & thoughts last Thursday morning (18 January: coincidentally my birthday), telephonically urging that, as you had just "taken over" my case from your predecessor (of whom I may say I did not have a high opinion: he was an ignorant, insensitive man & did not know that), & were also not yet familiar with Hamilton & environs (having relocated here from Toronto very recently), it would be "helpful" if I could communicate in writing what I thought might be "useful" for you to know, for our imminent relationship, I was not convinced that I could provide all that you want or anticipate, certainly not with sufficient conviction, clarity & detail (time is the enemy: my concentration & productivity are not what they were, & your deadline, next weekend (which will be, in practice, Sunday 28 January), although perhaps flexible, is intimidating); &, to be honest, I felt initially somewhat annoyed, thinking that you were expecting me to do some of your well-remunerated professional work for you! However, I have decided to do my best in the circumstances; if only to convince you that I will not need your ministrations for long.

Thinking further about it, I also decided to use your request as an opportunity to set up an experiment, for my own information, satisfaction & possible improvement. You see, as you may already have begun to perceive, I am a rather pedantic man (or so many of my colleagues & employees would have complained to you when I was daily complicating their lives); indeed, I was regarded by many of them, I am sure, as pedantic, petulant & pettifogging; a "control-freak", to use contemporary slang (other appropriate adjectives that may occur to you as you peruse my file & this document are: vain, egotistical, obsessive, voyeuristic: a normal human male, you may be thinking, Madam? - I assume you are something of a Feminist, as most professional women are, these benighted days; I wonder if you are married, and, if so, happily married?) .

(To give you an example of my urge for precision & order: Consider the dating above the title of this document: the order of a date is, & must always be, logically: first, day; second, month; third, year: any other order was unacceptable to me during my working years, to the chagrin of my secretaries, & still is in this my retirement and approaching dotage: I could never tolerate, for example, "Jan 21st 2001", since that is so obviously disordered, illogical, disheveled; & "01/21/01" or "01/01/21" would provoke a day's fury: I hope you understand & approve; if you do not, I promise you violent arguments when we meet! - which will be soon, I expect & hope.)

However, perhaps I am changing more than I have yet recognized (certainly the world is changing wildly all round me: indeed, however one defines its inauguration, we are now proceeding at a dizzying speed into the New Millenium ("Millennium"? - one is allowed to spell that impossible word wrongly!)): a strange event occurred just this morning (Sunday 21 January) - & it would normally have disturbed me greatly. I was in church (itself a strange event, the putative cause of which I shall relate in due course) when I noticed that the date offered by my watch (22 January; & yes, I am glad you noted that: I do consult my watch with obsessive frequency) did not accord with the date on the Communion Service bulletin; the latter advertising the correct date, but I could not of course ascertain that immediately, lacking requisite ancillary facts, & I was so disturbed & disoriented by this contradiction in dates that I asked my neighbor (who was charmingly & apparently uncritically responsive) what today's date was (is); but it remains a mystery for me that my watch (an expensive one that has never let me down before) proposes the wrong date; which it still does (I've just checked; of course I'll have to adjust it tomorrow, & have made a mental note to that effect; but it irks me to be displaying an erroneous date on my wrist). I mention these trivial events because they may nevertheless be significant in providing insight into my personality & situation (for a psychiatric therapist attempting to know what & whom she is dealing with, I mean; otherwise I would not mention them).

In the recent past (even, it occurs to me, three days ago!) I would have been extremely upset by the incident in church, would have been distracted throughout the service or been forced to depart, would have needed to find out (from a watchmaker, although I doubt if one exists in our computerized age) how the watch's erroneous date occurred & *when* it occurred (I would have wanted to know whether I have been misled about dates for a week, or a month, or merely today; even though that signifies little in my presently reclusive lifestyle); yet this morning, in the church of my father, St Paul's Anglican Church, Westdale, Hamilton, I found myself metaphorically shrugging and actually smiling; telling myself (and believing myself), that it really did not (it still does not) matter - & that the mystery is welcome to remain a mystery! For me, Madam my Therapist, that is momentous! Moreover, it accords with the spirit of this day, & also seems to portend acceptance of change in my life, & especially of one practical change that I have been considering for four years, in fact from the day after my wife died (23 December 1996): to sell this house in which I have lived for ten years (almost exactly ten years!), this mansion, this mausoleum, this secondary mental asylum; & move close to the center of Hamilton. (I have even looked at some quite satisfactory town-houses.) Yes, I shall restart that process; I shall move away from Ancaster. (I would have no difficulty in selling this house for an excellent price, now that the recession is over: &, as you will discover when you get to know your new city & its environs, mine is a select, "upscale", even "exclusive" neighborhood, inhabited by the rich & reclusive; although its status has been marred slightly (can one "mar" a status? - but let that pass) by the disappearance, in mysterious circumstances, of a neighbor, one McGregor, who is still, it seems, being pursued in all the corners of the world, although (as I overheard a few days ago when shopping for provisions in a local store) some of my fellow-citizens surmise that he has fled to a remote South Sea island, others that he now resides at the bottom of Hamilton's murky harbor, encased in cement, company for a local Mafia chief whose domain that has long been reputed to be; however, the notoriety consequent on Mr McGregor's flamboyant exit may even raise the price of my dwelling (or the whole episode may have been forgotten by the time my house appears on the market next Spring, the public memory being so extremely limited)).

(I apologize for all my parentheses, & especially for the double parentheses; if I I have time, energy and continuing inclination, I may remove them, for stylistic improvement, together with this paragraph, since it will then be irrelevant, in revision: Yes, I am a stickler for correctness in all communication, certainly comprehending orthography, syntax & punctuation! (Keep far from me all who do not know the difference between "who" and "whom", "whose" and "who's", "uninterested" and "disinterested"! Or confuse the colon with the semi-colon!) The current failure to respect apostrophes I find maddening; a sad commentary on the state of education in Ontario if not the entire English-speaking world. I am reminded of a grafitto I once saw on the London Underground: "Abolish Apostrophe's"; clearly inscribed by a pedant & purist after my own heart; maddened to laughter in his pain! However, you will have noted that I favor the ampersand (&) - in fact, adore the ampersand! Flowingly beautiful in itself, it has such a functional desirability as abbreviating the ubiquitous conjunction that I wish there were a similar replacement for "but". My use of the ampersand is not, then, as a colleague once tried to convince me, "mere affectation", but, used consistently, a contribution to the improvement of communication. I hope you agree!)

But I must outline my great experiment. (One of my life-long frustrations has been the knowledge that one can never contain all experience, even one's own mite of it, in one's mind, let alone in written words; which take so much time to set on the page, even with the aid of a word-processor (that word infuriates me, by the way: word-processors do *not* process words; words process *them*, & us!), that they can at best record events ever-receding half-known, barely-understood, never-comprehended, into the dim past (one spends one's life running, with increasing despair, after one's own life!) (Message to God: I do not approve of the fact that what I write now I would not have written yesterday, & could not write tomorrow; & that You, Sir, place us humans in this unacceptable state of interminable terminal uncertainty & tension that we call life; that you condemn us to the past even as we struggle to endure in the present; that we will never be able to understand, let alone express, our own reality, our Being; & then You have us die, You just cast us on Your junkheap (which some call Heaven, others Hell). All of us idiosyncratic individuals, all of us condemned to walk the same path, perform the same rituals of daily life - sleeping, waking, eating, drinking, shitting, pissing, fucking (those admirably explicit onamatopoeic Anglo-Saxon words!) - as we collectively journey on the same "quest" - for What? - gazing in horror at the same Waste Land. No, I do not approve; & yes, I know, You do not care what I think, Ultimate Sir.)

Order! What I decided was that I would immediately set three days as a period of action & analysis: and try to record and reflect upon the significant events therein, together with my responses in thought & emotion, as accurately & as fully as possible. My personality in a nutshell! - or that as the ideal. This endeavor expresses & accords with my lifelong commitment to scientific method as basic to any true understanding of actuality (I was trained to be a scientist, as the documents in my file might have informed you, & thereafter applied scientific principles in my careers (successfully productive, even somewhat eminent) as inventor, businessman & politician: you do not know it, but daily you use a small but lucrative invention of mine which unobtrusively simplifies your life & leaves you with more time to waste; & I would be surprised if you have not at least heard of my success in establishing and managing a major business in this city, a success acknowledged within the last decade of the deceased century in names chosen for two public buildings, & in receiving some credit for my achievements as a cabinet minister in an Ontario Government more intelligent & enlightened in its first term than its (disastrous!) second, though of course it claimed adherence to the same policies & intentions; but (unintentionally of course!) I boast).

Order! Order! My chosen period began last Friday (19 January, the day after your telephone-call) & ended today, Sunday (date above, not on my wrist!). I found on the first day that it would be helpful to my memory to carry a notebook & jot down occasionally what I experienced, & I shall rely on my notes as I compose this report during the next few days, trying to recall what has been a surprising, challenging & finally exhilarating succession of experiences. As I compose this paragraph, near the end of the experiment, I feel I have never been more alive! A statement that almost shocks me as I type it here on my computer. Can it be true, can I justify it?

Order! Order! Order!

2   MY PARENTS

To begin at the beginning; or before my beginning, since obviously my parents & their personalities, even the conjunction that produced me, occurred before I existed or was even conceived! I am the sole child of Arthur & Harriet Smith (though that surname is not, as you will immediately note, the one I now use: I changed my name legally, when I decided, at the age of twenty-nine, to cut myself free of what my father had become; my mother would have been mortified, but was deceased by then (mortified to excess, one might say!): she had suffered grievously from him, as had I). My father was a War Hero, a Canadian War Hero, & latterly a drunken sot; never choose to be born the only son of a War Hero! He tormented my poor mother into ill-health (she died in 1972, fourteen years before he did). I managed to escape, or partially escape (one could never entirely escape the memory of those beatings & other humiliations), because my mother had inherited enough money to send me to Upper Canada College & then to University (she was very proud of my academic success).

My father was born in 1914 & grew up a younger son on a farm near Cayuga; the Second World War arrived in time to inspire him & many of his friends; so, in 1940, full of heroic ideals & ambitions, he rushed off to join the Air Force & become Canada's second Billy Bishop; but instead found himself dropping bombs from a very great height onto the hapless, helpless citizenry (almost immediately to be kindled into ex-citizenry) of Hamburg and Dresden; achievements he would never talk about after the War; but his descent into anger & alcoholism talked silently on his behalf. He was not a good father to me, & I was not a good son to him. He hurt me, & eventually I hurt *him* even more, I think, by showing how much contempt I felt for him; that I despised him; hated him. Why am I telling you this? The answer will emerge below (I have added this section subsequent to experiences described later in this Report).

My mother was sweet, retiring & easily intimidated, as middle-class women of that generation generally were, & so was ineffectual; she could give me no protection when my father came home in his drunken rages, & *I* couldn't, or didn't, defend *her*; we both endured dumbly, & hated (hated *him*, yes, but eventually each other too, I think, because of our failure to help each other). She was a great reader, however, a lover of words, a poet who never even thought of writing poetry (perhaps I'm exaggerating there!); she loved words, & that at least I inherited from her and her example, for she found some refuge in her reading & crossword puzzling, & I have found pleasure in words too. (Do *you* have favorite words? I do; many, many; especially words whose meaning & phonetic structure collude, so that they *are* what they signify (if only humans were made like that!). *Tomb* is a current favorite (not just the vowel; how I love that B!), *complexity, stalwart, phantasmagoria*: a random few! Also, don't ask me why, but any word beginning IN: *inestimable, intrinsic, inimical, inherent, infinite* ... But back to work!)

(This morning's *Spectator* informs us, largely by alarmist headline, that our region is being flooded with fake $100-notes! The banks must be shivering in their billion-dollar vaults; businessmen on their way to work in stretch-limos must be quivering with rage & fear (especially now that, as the newspapers are also warning, the Economic Miracle is over & we are entering another Recession); even blind beggars in James Street must be spitting on $100-notes casually placed in their bowls. What I am leading up to, Madam my Therapist, is that you, as you peruse this Communication (*are* you perusing it, or merely allowing your eyes to exercise themselves with my precious lifeblood on this once-virgin page?), is the warning that you should be aware that much, most, perhaps *all* of what you read in this Report is the verbal equivalent of a bank-vault stuffed with $100-notes which may or may not be fake.)

I am writing these words on a grey chilly morning (I say "chilly" only on the evidence of opening the front-door & retrieving (why not "trieving"?) this morning's harvest of newspapers). As I sit here in my "office", I hear you saying, in my memory, "Write what you like. However you like. Write what you're thinking. What you're feeling. Your opinions. Your ideas. Your feelings." (I apologize for the repetitive sentence-fragments, but they were yours & I am merely reporting them.) Of course it is impossible to do what you requested. What I am writing is words, words, words that may or may not communicate to you what I may *have been* thinking, feeling, etc, or *thinking* that I was thinking, feeling, etc: & then you may or not be able to receive, comprehend, interpret any meanings those words may or may not "contain" or have been intended to "contain". "That way madness lies"? Exactly: we *are* all mad, are we not? (But it is important that we (that is., you and I) understand each other!)

(Early this morning I was writing some words you have already read (& also some I exterminated more or less immediately), to this effect: You will know from information in my file that I go to bed (not, alas, necessarily to sleep) at eight p.m., then rise at four a.m. "Why?" It is a habit; but it pleases me, consoles me, to retire when others are out & about, & then to be moving & doing when they are not; to be active when they are inactive; to be present when they are absent; to have the transient but repeated illusion of being the only being in existence; to be uniquely, solely alive; that, at least, is my rationalization! (I do not always sleep so programmatically, alas!) This morning I sat for a moment surrounded by the usual somnolent silence & then switched on the computer; it hummed companionably; the screen glowed; & I started communicating. I wrote also then (& then obliterated my words) about Change.

For you, as for your predecessor, Change is Gain; every therapist, every psychiatrist with whom I have had dealings has preached Change as Gain. But what about Change as Pain? Move, you all say to me, openly or by insinuation; Move away, Move on, Move forward. Move, move, move! But I have lived in this house, *my* house, for ten years! Sometimes, I look around my home, & think that it is (or has become) a prison (is this a type of prison-diary I am composing, I wonder?); at other times, I gaze at this sofa & that painting, & think "These are my friends; they are my company of saints". How could I begin selling them? How could I pack the unsold remnants & transport them to where they do not belong, & never will belong? Above all, this house is my Taj Mahal; for it is Elaine's home too: she is all around me, she breathes beside me, she has her being here. How could I leave her? Yet you will say "Go, fare forward": Move. I will not, I cannot.)

So much for my parentage - though I see I have fared far beyond that topic! What may that portend? (I may later return and assassinate that whole delinquent paragraph, or at least restore order to this item!)

3   MY WIVES

Shall we play Happy Families? Yes, Madam my Therapist, I *am* being ironic. In the file, you will have perused the information that I have been married thrice; divorced twice; & fathered four children (eight, actually, if one counts those born out of wedlock (two) or aborted (one), and the one, in wedlock, who died in early infancy (for more information about one of those born out of wedlock, & now deceased, see Item 4 below). Of course those facts do not suggest marital & familial bliss; but I hasten to say that, unlike my father (and, it seems, my son), I did not ever strike a woman or a child; though I was the one who walked out of my first two marriages ("Honesty, honesty!" pleads my conscience - My Lord, the statement is factually true; but yes, I walked out only after my sexual misdemeanors (in common parlance, affairs) were discovered by the two relevant wives, so that you could say my evacuations were, at best, pre-emptive, recognitions of the inevitable; at worst, expressions of anger & cowardice). Did I "love" my first two wives? I thought so at the time. There was even some enjoyable sex, though they were both somewhat reticent women; &, amusingly, they had similarities that included their looks (both "shapely blondes", you might say) & the facts that one could never finish a sentence (maddening!) & the other could never close a door or switch off a light (maddening!); I wondered afterwards how I had managed to suppress my irritation long enough to sire two children each with them (for my families, see below, Item 6).

You asked me to ask myself whether (I hope I quote you accurately) I "have a hole in my life" (an ugly phrase, but a forceful one!). Oh yes, there are many holes in my life; & in my head; & in my heart, Madam my Therapist; I leak pain & self-pity (you see, I *am* trying to be honest!). One controls what he can control in his life; then one finds that he can't control any of it after all; & other people mess up what's left! So, ultimately, it all collapses, disintegrates, sifts into dust & disorder. That's what happened to me just over four years ago, on 23 December 1997 to be precise, when my wife Elaine died. That event inaugurated my crisis: I fell into that hole at the center of my life, down, down, down into darkness; into what they laughingly call depression ("Depression"! - as if they just had to raise the lid & you would pop merrily back into your life like a grinning Jack-in-the-Box!). The 1997-98 Holiday Season (how I hate the term *Holiday* now!) transmogrified into the slippery edge of Hell: I drank copiously at the funeral, said I was "Fine, fine, fine"; they drove me home, assorted family members, & I insisted they leave me there, "Yes, I'm fine, just go, please, go"; & the Furies descended upon me from a louring sky & tore me apart utterly; I drank, drank, drank, drank, I fell dead, rose from the dead, ran naked & screaming down the icy streets until the police, summoned by my neighbors (an act of kindness, perhaps, but I never thought of thanking them for it, since they were also protecting the value of their houses), escorted me to the oblivion of a mental hospital. That was merely the start of my sufferings; I was Job without patience & trust in God; I was Christ crucified, incognito. Is that blasphemous? Should I care? Oh, I suffered, I suffered, & the darkness seemed illimitable; with intervals of lucidity & hope; & then another breakdown; & another. The world receded; I was an empty shell left by the tide on the endless beach. Yet: I am not now as I was then; I am recovered, or half-recovered (your predecessor said so!); I am raised from the dead. The ministrations of such as you, & the medication I suck into my veins at regular intervals, have made it possible to stand now on the edge of the precipice; the fiery furnace licks at my feet, but my mouth breathes air not smoke, my eyes stare at stars not blackness, my ears hear angelic harmonies not the shrieking of fiends. ("Show-off!" you are thinking, aren't you? "Melodramatic stuff & nonsense," huff huff! But you have not been where I have been, Madam my Therapist; none of you have! - you only observe, analyze, come to conclusions that are at best clever guesses. But *I* was *there!*)

Of course suffering is endemic in this world; it surrounds us, like the sea, waves of the sea. Children suffer, the old suffer; the poor suffer, multitudes of the Third World suffer, even prosperous middle-aged Canadians have been known to suffer; & there is nothing any human can do to end our suffering; it is ordained, it is inevitable, it is our Fate. Suffering can, I acknowledge, be ameliorated, reduced. But do we really want it to be? In the news of the last few days, a Nigerian teenage girl is flogged barbarically for being forced to have sex with three men & bearing the baby of one of them; a common-law couple is charged, here in The Best Country in the World, with beating their baby girl to death; our daily newspaper headlines the mistreatment of fostered children; babies are sold, & resold, on the Internet - & from the Saturday front pages of the three newspapers I take, though I don't get time to read them except cursorily (the *Hamilton Spectator* for local news, the *Globe and Mail* for national and international news, the *National Post* because I'm curious & believe in competition - will the latter two cut each others' throats, or, as I predict, prosper, like Coke & Pepsi, by clawing at each other; the latter outcome would suit me doctrinally & even justify some of my more intelligent political speeches) the sad eyes of Robert Latimer peer, peer into our souls ("Life Sentence Upheld"; he will spend at least ten years, unless our shabby shiftless Federal Government decides to confer clemency on him, for the mercy-killing of his severely-disabled twelve-year-old daughter: poor Tracy, God gave you a life of pain, poor poor Robert, God gave you the compassion & the strength (& responsibility?) to end it (why is it that we are compas-

sionate to suffering animals, yet turn our minds away from euthana-
sia, from giving suffering children a merciful death?). (You see, Robert
Latimer took *responsibility*, he decided what he could do to ameliorate
suffering & he *did* it, & told us all, willingly, what he did, how he did
it; & took & takes the consequences. Is that not heroism? But we are
uncomfortable with heroes, especially Canadian heroes. So, of course
R.L. is right: we want to forget him as soon as we can, for he is also our
sacrifice, our comfortable alibi. But look, Canada, into his eyes, & see
yourselves at your compassionate suffering defeated best! See *heroism*.
Then hang your heads in shame.)

So how dare I hope to avoid suffering? Well, I did not avoid suffering (perhaps I didn't pray hard or often enough?), & I know that
my increasing & finally intense happiness during the three days of my
Great Experiment will ensure that when my suffering returns, it will be
the deeper, harsher, even the more impossible to endure. That, after all,
is God's plan for us: one damn thing after another so that we tolerate
present pain, boredom, despair, in the expectation of the bliss, or at
least relief, of the next orgasm; & a consummately successful plan it is,
if you put a premium on continuity! Take Sex. (Yes, we all say, Yes, yes!
I'll take it! - which conclusively demonstrates the success of God's little
arrangement.) You'll agree (Feminist that you undoubtedly are!) with
my next observation: Every man is essentially a Penis seeking its next
orgasm. Goodbye, Clinton; but you were right to make exceedingly
light of being sucked-off by a pretty & ambitious intern under your
Oval Office executive table: you know what I know, that every man,
any man, would welcome it; that, at any moment of consciousness, we
are ready for it, seeking it, begging for it, doing it solo if there's noone
to do it with, for or to us: the next orgasm, the orgasm that will leave
us slavering for the next orgasm, & the next, & the next. Are women
not like that too? How it would help if we would take that insight,
that truth, into politics, into that egotists' playground of interminable evasion and hypocrisy. I'm composing this on the day that English
Canada is fulminating over the deliberately-provocative remark of one
Bernard Landry, due to inherit the mantle of Lucien Bouchard as leader of the Parti Quebecois, that the Canadian flag, the sacred Maple
Leaf, is (quote) a Piece of Red Rag!!! "Shock-horror" blare our one-
day-wonder English media - newspapers & radio & television; giving
him just what he craves, his orgasm of the day. So why don't we think
of it that way and save a lot of ugly fulminating: it was merely his next
orgasm, & now the Federal Government, the Opposition, are enjoying
their next orgasm, & so are we, & so are they, & so on, & so on? Well,

it's one way to hold a country together; an enjoyable & natural way, when you think about it, all of us having fun, orgasm after orgasm, Canada as the Ejaculation of Ejaculations! - & none of us, in orgasm, committing violence against each other, in word or deed. Can't we just concentrate on enjoying the situation; have as many orgasms as we can before the last one (which is called Death); & thank God for it? No? But see, it's a Divine way of running our affairs! Are we just too stupid to recognize that?

Have you decided that I am crazy, Madam my Therapist? Or are you withholding judgement, in the approved scientific way? Be careful, now! Dispassionate objectivity is all. You shouldn't dislike me before you have even met me!

It is now over a year since I was last incarcerated in the HPH (I realize that the Hamilton Psychiatric Hospital is now, in consequence of an amalgamation process, officially designated St. Joseph's Mountain Healthcare, but it was the HPH when it was my temporary home, so I am not being merely pedantic!). Is that nightmare finally over? I hardly dare hope so. (This past Christmas and New Year were the first since 1997 when I succeeded in controlling my pain, my depression, & so did not cause any fracas or commotion that would have provoked my neighbors to call the police, & the police to deposit me in the HPH for further temporarily-effectual treatment.) (Not that they have yet sent a deputation to thank me for my civic forbearance!)

What has changed, then, if anything? (For change is always about us too: in the past few days, we have fed on news regarding the exit of three Presidents in three very different nations and in very different ways: Clinton in the United States of America; Estrada in the Philippines; Kabila in the Congo. Yes, while there is change there is hope, they say: another dimension of the game God plays with us, keeping us in survival mode, holding down the suicide rate, throwing us a bone of optimism just as we starve towards despair.) Well, what has changed in my life? So much, so little. Let me tell you, briefly, about my marriages. Of my three wives, only the final one, Elaine, gave me the love & support that I needed; I yearn for her still, I hear her voice in the next room, I see her shadow at the back door. We had no children; not only because we were rather too old for that when we married, but because we didn't want any; because we were self-sufficient. It was for her that I built this house; we planned it together, watched it being built together, furnished it together; we were happy beyond all I could ever have imagined. I do not wish to say more about Elaine, & our relationship. She was the light of my life; I miss her intolerably and always will. Her death was sudden (pancreatic cancer); so I was deprived of what North Americans now consider their birthright, Closure; and no doubt that is part of what I have been seeking ever since, and will never find. (I do not believe in Closure, which is a costly, extravagant delusion that no earlier civilizations sought, and that no other culture or society in our time is stupid and pampered enough to seek.)

My first two marriages were disastrous (as I have already revealed above), although productive of two pairs of female children (one pair twins). I do not blame my wives for those marital failures. As I have said, I was responsible to the extent that I philandered. (Let me confess here that, apart from the discovered affairs, I had several short-term relationships and even used prostitutes on occasion (when staying at hotels, on business-trips, for instance, or overnight in Toronto more recently).) Both wives seem distant now, though I have occasionally bumped into them over the years, and had amicable conversations with them; Jayne remarried and for that reason, perhaps, seems more forgiving than my first wife, Caroline. Of course, at my daughters' weddings (three of them are married) I played the part of Father of the Bride, smilingly unctuous and utterly photogenic; and, until my breakdown in 1997, I tried to remain on friendly terms, where possible, with both families; attending christenings when invited, remembering birthdays, etc. So am I a model ex-husband? Well, I tried. But even the four children seem distant to me now; and my five grandchildren are small strangers.

4   MY SON

Nobody (except you from the moment of reading this) knows that I have a son. I have pondered this revelation; wondering whether to make it conditional on your never divulging what I will now tell you; but I have decided against that, for more than one reason: that you requested utter truth, that it may help my future state of mind to confess it now (put that first: selfish reasons are always primary, primal!); that - I thought there was another reason in my mind, but, if so, it has concealed itself. His name was Derek. He has been in the news quite recently, especially in Hamilton, so you may remember what he did: killed a little boy, the son of the woman he had been living with (she was fortunate to survive), and a few days later his naked body was found, covered with snow, on a ski-trail some distance from a summer-cottage which he had broken into. Those are the bare facts, culled from media reports; I know little else & do not wish to. Coincidentally, his mother's death was announced in the *Spectator* on the same day that the murder was reported, Monday 8 January.

I must now explain how I know he is my son (his surname is not mine), & what he means, & has meant, in my life. The story is quite complicated, but I shall simplify it. His mother, Margaret, was a woman I had an affair with during my first marriage (Caroline, my first wife, never knew about that affair, & it had nothing to do with the collapse of our marriage, which was precipitated by a subsequent affair with my then-Secretary). I did not know that Margaret was pregnant at the time we separated & she left Hamilton; & she never told me, even though she returned to Hamilton five years later, after marrying a widower with two children; she never told me that she had borne my child, my only son; she never told me that my son existed! It was only when he was in his teens that I discovered his existence. Her uncle, who had been our neighbor when Caroline & I lived in downtown Hamilton, told me, but only as a secret; he was in financial difficulty & begged me for a loan; & after I'd agreed & we were having a drink together, he said he had something on his conscience: he had always felt, although sworn to secrecy, that I should have been told that when Margaret left Hamilton, saying she didn't love me any longer, she was in fact pregnant with my son. I was stunned. He was reluctant to give me more information, & at the time I persuaded myself I should not follow the matter further; after all, I was married again, to Jayne, & she was expecting our second child, which I hoped would be a boy. A year or so later, I asked Tom for more information, & soon even saw the birth certificate (I had my connections, remember, being an MPP at Queen's Park by then); it did not identify me as the father; in fact, Margaret had written "Not Known" in the "Father" column, & she gave him *her* surname. I still remember the astonishment & then the intense anger, the fury, I felt when I saw that. For one of the few times in my life, I was truly enraged; I thought I would have to strike somebody, anybody. How could she do that to me? Whatever she had come to feel about me, whatever made her change her mind, she had told me often how much she loved me; & I *was* the Father! - you can't change a fact like that. It was total dishonesty; total betrayal. I thought of facing her with that, confronting her - she was in Hamilton, married, as I said, to a man I even knew slightly, having done business with him (in fact, he had used my invention in one of his company's products); & I had even seen her once or twice, with his two children, once walking downtown with them (I was driving home, stopped at a light, & they crossed right in front of me); but I changed my mind; it wasn't worth the risk of disrupting my family life, & the publicity could have been damaging (especially as I was already under attack by the Opposition for a speech proposing legislation to reduce, slightly, welfare payments to single mothers: in the light of the present Ontario Government's policies and practices, a merely minuscule proposal of economic good sense and social reconstruction in a period of necessary restraint after aeons of sentimental socialistic excess; at most a political peccadillo, Madam, so do restrain your fury!)

So (to resume) I decided, instead, to seek out my son myself: my son Derek, whom I had never seen. He must have been about fifteen when I first saw him. It was on Locke Street. I knew immediately it was him. I'd found out, I forget how, that he would often be there; hanging out, as they say, with a group of friends, in the late afternoon. And yes, there he was, with a group of skateboarders, four of them, one a girl; he was their leader, swooping down the sidewalk, right past my car. I felt like reaching out the window & catching hold of him as he passed. I knew he was my son the moment I saw him. Vigorous, handsome, every inch my son! And the girl right behind him: yes, he was already sexually active; I could see it in her adoring eyes. Next day I waited in a coffee shop, and when I saw him I stepped out and forced a minor collision; berated him mildly for skateboarding on the sidewalk; then told him I had a nephew who was interested in skateboarding etcetera - there's no need to go into all the detail; suffice it to say that I watched him skateboarding at a park once or twice (how I admired his ability to surge up the ramp, reach up into the air, high, high, hang there, twist, swing down & sweep triumphantly away; I reveled in his vitality & talent, the way he challenged & conquered danger!) I told him I'd like to buy him a new skateboard & any new clothes he'd like, so we went together to a sports store in Dundas & I encouraged him to choose whatever appealed to him. Yes, he did try, in a desultory way, to find out about me, who I was, why I was interested in him; but I parried with easy lies, & soon he just accepted my occasional beneficent presence in his life; just another admirer. I'm sure he never suspected anything - no doubt Margaret had told him her husband was his father; at any rate, he just took me as I came, swallowing my lies, casually accepting anything I gave him, my tributes. But I became aware that he was already drinking (the newspaper reports state that he was a chronic alcoholic by the time of his death, & I saw the beginnings of that, smelled liquor on his breath); I also sensed that he was deeply unhappy, though he masked that with bravado. What should I have done? What *could* I have done? For him, I mean. I was aware that I was taking a great risk; that I might be seen by someone who knew me & would tell Margaret.

At the same time, my anger against Margaret had intensified: that she, who had concealed my fatherhood, was neglecting our son, allowing him to roam the streets, to get involved in alcohol & possibly drugs & who knows what else!

What did happen, though, was that I was summoned unexpectedly to the Premier's office; the Minister of Welfare had just resigned, due to ill-health, & I was offered the job! (My speech about the desirability of reducing welfare payments for single mothers, so as to discourage their immoral, destructive lifestyle, had impressed the Party's business supporters, and there was need to shore up support as an election was imminent.) My immediate acceptance, & all of its complex aftermath, preoccupied me for months; & when I had time & energy to think about Derek again, I realized it was now impossible for me to resume any connection with him. Or *was* it impossible? Now I look back & wonder if I was right; but that's the way it looked at the time: a social & political necessity. So now I was out of his life, & he was out of mine; & perhaps we had never connected in any deep way. Did he miss me at all? I doubt it. Did I miss him? I don't think so; never had time to. But perhaps, somewhere deep down - one of those holes in my life?

Anyway, I moved on. Other affairs with women (power, even my minor portion of it, is an aphrodisiac, of course - I was besieged!); a second divorce (which attracted a temporary negative publicity after Jayne gave a vindictive interview); & then Elaine. But when I saw in the *Spectator* (or heard on the CBC News, I can't recall which was first) that Derek had attacked a woman & her child, both so severely that they were not expected to live - well, I was shocked; of course I was shocked. You see, I hadn't thought about him for many years; the years in the Government, the years with Elaine; or at least, I don't think I ever thought of him; but occasionally I would dream of a boy on a skateboard, flying high between the sun & my blinded eyes; & if I remembered the dream at all (usually just the very edge of it), I was yearning for him to land, come down to earth, but knew he never would - & then I woke filled with a searing, soaring anguish.

I was glad to read that he committed suicide. There was some speculation that he had been killed somehow & stripped of his clothes; no doubt the truth will never be known. But I prefer to think he killed himself by going out into the winter naked. I wasn't sure *why* I was glad, though. All this happened only weeks ago, & I'm still turning it over in my mind. There are several obvious reasons, of course: relief, for him, that he won't face trial & lifelong imprisonment (I must add that I have always argued for the death penalty, that if you take another's life, you forfeit your own); relief, too, for myself, that I won't feel any need to reconnect with him, when I could no longer do anything to help him - if indeed I ever could. Relief, yes. But emotions beyond that which I can't yet identify, & which trouble me. Admiration, pride, exhilaration? - that my son had done what he should have done; what a man should do; that he had proved himself so absolutely my son in his death (many of us are hurt in childhood & youth, but we none of us have the right to use that as an excuse for hurting anybody else; that I believe utterly). Perhaps I will in time be able to identify more completely what I feel.

Of course my reaction has been complicated by the simultaneous news of Margaret's death. What can I say about how I feel about that? Turmoil, again, turmoil. You see, I did love her. Until I met Elaine, Margaret was the love of my life. In so many ways, I recognized that more clearly as I grew older; Elaine was very like Margaret; & both had characteristics in common with my Mother; their voices, for instance; low and soft. I could not bear it when Margaret rejected me; I wouldn't accept it; how dare she say that! - do that! - when we both knew how much we loved each other! Going away so abruptly into silence, as she did, may have saved my marriage, for a while; but ultimately it also destroyed my marriage, both my first two marriages, because, in a way, I think I went on looking for her. And it almost destroyed *me*. Do you understand what I'm saying? Because I don't think I do, fully. And I hate any mystery or uncertainty. (But psychiatrists are wise, aren't they? Trained to put Humpty Dumpty back together again. Do you really want to try to put me together again? "A hole in my life"? My whole life is a hole (the pun is unbearable; I'll remove it; language can be cruel, can torture us). I have fallen into it - this black bottomless pit, down, down, down. Soon, surely, I must hit bottom.)

(26 January: How does one begin to make sense of, bring order to, comprehend the plethora, the phantasmagoria which is Life? Here I sit, a week after I commenced composing this Report, trying to provide you with even the simplest information about my life, the most superficial insight into my (complex? - would you agree with that by now?) personality & experience, while the world slams at me from every angle, complicating what is already complicated beyond human endurance. Yes, the poet said it, I remember: "Humankind cannot bear too much reality"; yes, but what else is there to bear, Sir? - the suffering, the occasional joy, the orgasms, the daily parody that is the experience of each existence, all are merely passing moments in Your great plan which we grimacingly call Reality! Anyway, to proceed (or recede? -

annoying, that orthographical discrepancy!): From the morning's CBC news, I learned that the High Court is due to pronounce on the nation's catastrophic Possession of Pornography Act. What will the learned ladies and gentlemen come up with this time in their futile attempt to incarcerate the penises of the nation? Children must be protected; that I concede: but not at the expense of imprisoning the rest of us! I confess that I have viewed pornographic videos, many of them, in my private residence; & indeed I still possess a few, although I have not viewed one for years (not since I married Elaine, in fact). The argument against Gun Registration is similarly cogent: Don't tell me how to run my life, don't interfere in my private business! Your law cannot succeed, cannot control human nature; you will only release other demons! (Are *you* a Bleeding Heart, Madam, my Therapist? No doubt, or why would you become a therapist, that impossible animal? If so, you are now reading the words of The Enemy, the unreconstructed Male Conservative Bastard, who will resist to the end your puny attempts at social engineering!) Gun Registration will not stop unlawful killing by gun, since those who will rob & murder were beyond & ahead of the law in the first place. Similarly, viewing pornography does not cause violence (rape, child sexual abuse); in fact, it provides a safety-valve; it *saves* children from harm. Those who commit violence must be punished, of course; they must take responsibility. In giving them excuses (like the right to blame pornography & parents), society merely intensifies the danger that the innocent face from evil-doers. (I think I'm recycling a campaign speech; sorry. Let it end here.) (I almost add now: "Let it all end here." But I didn't. So?)

5   MARGARET

(But I think I've said all I need to, or want to, about her in the item above. Anyway, I don't wish to resume writing on such a painful topic. When I revise this report, I'll do the thing with flinging paragraphs around, and deposit her here, where she belongs!)

6   MY OTHER CHILDREN

Madam my Therapist, it is a bright cold day as I continue this Report; brilliantly sunny, but extremely cold (minus-ten, I think, is the predicted maximum for today; but we've had so few sunny days this winter that this one is a palpable relief); through my window I look across a frozen sea of iced snow, beautiful at a distance, to a line of firs beyond. But - interruptions, interruptions! (Your sentence-fragments are catching!) (It was interruptions that helped to end my political career! I was so weary of requests for favors, demands for information, challenges to respond to questionnaires, by the end! One could hardly find time for the work one had been elected to perform! Although I was a Minister of some prominence, & even whispered of as a possible successor to the Premier if he ever decided to step down, I decided, after marrying Elaine, that enough was enough. I wanted to spend more time with her. I wanted some peace! And, let me be honest, there were other reasons; there always are!) But even after my retirement from the political scene, people will not leave me in my desired reclusive state (I am often deliberately rude now, especially when telephonically attacked for contributions to this or that so-called charity): already this morning, I have been interrupted beyond endurance: *five* telephone calls, one from the estate-agent, who wanted to advertize my house & seemed to think I had committed myself to selling it (I told him that an advertisement would be premature; that I need more time to consider my position); & then a call from my eldest daughter, Anne, who invited me to lunch in a restaurant (she knows better than to suggest coming here; she said she needed to talk to me about a problem threatening her marriage, that she can't talk about it to her mother or anyone else, that it has to do with her husband, who, she eventually said, tearfully, is spending so much time away from her & the children that she is convinced he is having an affair); I was tempted to say that I am hardly the right person to give appropriate advice on such a matter, & that I know she also wants to talk to me because, like her sister and half-sisters, she would like to gauge my state of sanity (or insanity), &, if opportunity arises, find out how much they can expect to inherit when I pass on to my Reward in Heaven or Hell; but I merely said that, Yes, she could pick me up, I'd be happy to have lunch with her; & I heard, in the ensuing breathy silence, her amazement that she had succeeded, & so easily (I don't know why I caved in like that; uncharacteristic; but then, she is the child most like me in temperament; determined, egotistical, confident, direct). Then there was a call from your office, Madam, reminding me of our appointment at 10 a.m. on Wednesday 31 January (how could I forget?). And then there was a call from my housekeeper (yes, I have one; did you think I could possibly keep this mansion in good order, a comfortable tidy clean habitation for a retired inventor, businessman and politician?); she would not be able to come for a few days because she had been summoned to look after grandchildren, their mother being very ill. Finally a call from my doctor's office: could I come in for an appointment on Tuesday afternoon (30 Feb)? - Yes; how could I say No? Five calls, bursting through my meditative silence. Perhaps that is why I am beginning to feel tense.

Oh, this Item was to cover my four legitimate children: Anne, Elizabeth, & the twins, Meredith, Tracy. But I find I really don't have much to say. They are attractive young women (or so the husbands of the two still married must have thought) in their twenties or thirties, the prime of life; Anne, married to a lawyer (she is one herself), has three children; Meredith (in Toronto, a U of T professor recently divorced from a doctor) has two; Tracy, the most recently married (to an engineer), has no children yet, and is a primary-school teacher; only Elizabeth remains single - she is studying theology & is probably a lesbian. Do I sound bored, detached? The two mothers, my ex-wives, stand in the way of any affectionate connection with the children; I am, they all know, the father who abandoned them, who played a minor (mainly financial) role in their early lives. Did they ever "need" me? Well, now they are launched into their own worlds of change and chance, that is a merely theoretical question. There is also my illegitimate daughter; but she is now in Italy with her mother; I send her & the mother money at fairly regular intervals, & they seem content.

(Actually, I fear that the boredom relates also to this Report, which is becoming a burden I regret shouldering; but which I will complete, since I undertook it: I pride myself on keeping my word!). Duty, responsibility: standards now unpopular, especially with the young, who have no idea how privileged their lives are; but I believe in those standards & have tried to fulfil them throughout my life: the true businessman's ethic, I think, & a noble one, which I took into politics with me.)

7   MY QUEST: DAY ONE, FRIDAY 19 JANUARY 2001

Here we go! Or rather, there I did go; on Friday 19 January, a grey day (the sun muffled throughout). I woke up in the very early morning, not having slept well (mainly, I think, because of your call the previous day, my promise to write this Report for you, & then my decision to use the next three days as my great Experiment). So, after breakfast, I got into my car & just drove - started the engine, & drove. Where to? For the first time in my life, I think (& no doubt because I was so weary), I fell into a sort of trance; just drove, extemporizing my direction. I found myself driving down towards Hamilton, then turning along Dundurn, then east onto York Boulevard (the original route to Toronto), past the pretentious Victorian wedding-cake of Dundurn Castle; old, sprawling Hamilton Cemetery on my left; grey icy Lake on my right; over the bridge with its four high pillars - & only then did I become aware (allow myself to become aware?) of where I was going.

While Elaine was alive, we traveled that route often to the Arboretum of the RBG (the Royal Botanical Gardens: you must already know this glory of Hamilton, circling our corner of the Lake?). We would take her dog, Tiny Tim, there, for a walk, & in spring also wander through the Lilac Garden, bemused by the sheer voluptuous loveliness of blossom. Elaine & I would hold hands and stroll companionably; TT would romp about us, yanking at his lead: yes, that was happiness; it hurts now to remember it & record it. At the end of an old broad avenue of oaks, leading towards the Lake's westmost finger (Coote's Paradise that area's called), we would sit together on a bench below a big old tree; gaze south at a gallery of trees, & the Lake beyond them, & talk, talk, talk; TT lying at Elaine's feet. (He was *her* dog; after her death I had him put down because I could not bear to have him yearning at me.)

So now my quest began; there, where we had so often walked. I parked the car & picked my way cautiously & with some difficulty over the half-frozen snow pitted with fossilized footsteps (it would sustain me for a few steps, then suddenly give way, & my foot would jerk sharply down into softer snow; I feared putting my back out, but emerged unscathed!). When I reached our tree, I sat there on the bench (a new one, actually, replacing our familiar battered perch) for some ten minutes; a mysterious contentment beginning to seep through me (it was cold of course, but my coat & gloves kept me warm enough); as I left, I saw that a sign on it now identifies our tree as a "TULIP TREE or TULIPIER" (which reminded me of its pink summer blossom) & that a deep crack in its ribbed trunk runs right up to the sign. It is *our* tree, & always will be. Leaving the RBG, I was aware that I had begun a sort of pilgrimage. Where would it take me next?

Driving slowly back towards Hamilton, I noticed a cleared parking area beside the road & pulled into it. Iced snow was piled high beside the car (thrown up from the road by snowploughs over the past few weeks of heavy snowfalls) but I clambered up onto & over it somehow, & walked very slowly forward over a smooth, sometimes slippery surface, towards the lake; & there, ahead of me, reared my second destination: a large brown veined stone, silhouetted against the snow & the soft greyness beyond. I went up to it & read an inscription on a simple plaque: "Guard this resting place / of these unknown / soldiers, immigrants / & citizens / War of 1812-1814 / Ship-fever 1847-1848 / Cholera 1854-1815". How many died? Here, then, long years ago, they came to die; & in the cold wind I felt them, ghosts swirling protectively about me, gently touching my face. And now I think I began to know where my journey was taking me; & even though my final destination that morning was not, I think, yet in my consciousness, I felt resistance growing somewhere inside me.

Back at my car, I noticed a monument across the road: a flight of twelve steps up to a high ledge (once a gun-emplacement?) backed by the Lake to the east (Hamilton Harbor, & beyond that the elephantine bulk of Lake Ontario); why, in all my years in Hamilton, had I never before paid any attention to this simple sign at the top of the steps? I had passed it often enough; on our way to walk TT, for instance). The inscription memorialized one Thomas Baker McQuesten, 1882-1948 (yes, I had heard of him, vaguely - yes, his House, open to the public), "An influential proponent of landscape improvement" who, as the city's Parks Manager, as Ontario's Minister of Highways and as Chairman of the Niagara Parks Commission, "devoted himself to the development of parks and scenic parkways" - an eminent local & political predecessor whose creativity gives pleasure (& always will give pleasure) to all who live here, & protects the environment he so loved; including this view, which must have delighted him as it delights me. In fact, I believe he is credited with establishing the Royal Botanical Gardens, perhaps the greatest glory of Hamilton. As I stood there, I felt humbled & grateful; & thought how the dead live with us still in their beneficence, how we are surrounded by their achievements, the gifts of their talent & vigor. How the dead do not die. (Or did I merely inherit those worthy thoughts? I also thought how unworthy his successors, the local politicians of this area, including me, have been. But at least I did, in my time, try to argue that attention should be paid to the core of our city; that it could only thrive if we remembered that, like all cities, its core is commercial - of course you must make it possible for merchants, small-businesmen, to make a good living, must keep their taxes low enough, make sure that they could compete with the vast malls that now encircle the city like a great boa-constrictor, squeezing life out of it. And all they did, ineffectual pygmies, was plant marigolds & nasturtiums - imitating McQuesten rather than learning from him to do what needed to be done to preserve what needed to be preserved!) Below me, on the railway-line, a long train of wagons, rumbling & clanging behind an already-distant locomotive, was heading for the steel-mills; so many wagons (CP Rail, Uni-Pacific, CSX, TEM, GT, Conrail, NS, Canadian National, others already out of sight), most of them brown but one at least bright blue. Beyond, across the iced water, the stacks of Stelco & Dofasco belched smoke that drifted towards the Escarpment that protects & divides this city (I tried to count the chimneys & reached 20, but my sight is no longer sharp); two chimneys were emitting thick pulsing flame, dragons breathing out fire from the steel pyres of their lungs. (I'll be writing poetry soon, if I go on in this rhetorical style!)

When I got back into the car, I expected to head home; I wanted to; I was beginning to feel weary. But found myself crossing to the other side of the road (an illegal manoeuver, I know, but there was little traffic; the time was now 8:45). Then I was heading east again, in the direction of Toronto, & began to understand where my journey, my quest, was to culminate. I missed the turning I should have taken, just beyond the bridge (Valley Inn Road, it's called, narrow & winding, leading you down to another bridge, a single-track wooden bridge over a narrow reach of the bay); so I drove on towards Burlington, turning off at the road that leads to the main center of the RBG; passed those buildings & turned right towards my destination, Woodland Cemetery, which occupies a hilly bluff, a minor peninsula, rising sharply from the Lake & facing Hamilton across its bay. Yes, I knew now where I was going. Something within me was resisting strongly; but was encountering a stronger force; what I might now, in retrospect, call a need. (I am trying to explicate all this, Madam my Therapist, to facilitate your analysis; indeed, I am providing the analysis! You might find it strange, as I did; all this swirling subconscious activity in my scientific brain?) (It really did remind me of my boyhood struggles with masturbation: you knew it was evil (that appalling, & so unnecessary, burden of guilt loaded onto several generations of young males!), & you knew you would do it eventually, but meanwhile the hopeless battle between mind & body, "conscience" & physical urge.)

The Cemetery is a maze; and I had not been there for some fourteen years - to be exact, since 10 October 1986, the day my father was buried here; so I drove very slowly along the narrow curving roads until I came to the main military cemetery (Sections 5 and 5A, I noted); & I sat there for a while, in the warmth of my purring car, gazing at the serried ranks of grey headstones (how many? - at least a thousand, each with its inscribed cross) stretching ahead of me, and to my left, and to my right, row on row; enfolded by the protective beauty of a natural amphitheater; an army finally at rest. Again the air seemed to be replete with beneficent spirits, an emanation from the rich, generous earth that held their bones. Then, finally I felt strengthened, ready to go on, to encounter my Father. His grave is in the newer military cemetery (Section 18) created (it must have been) when the main one had been filled by the early 1980s. I was there when he was buried, though

I had not seen him for many years - & did not want to now, I thought. But then - why am I here?

In early October 1986, in my Queen's Park office, I received a telephone call from a young Anglican priest, a woman; to tell me that my father was dying and he had asked her to let me know that "He would like to see you, to say goodbye." She told me later, after the funeral, which she conducted, that he had attended communion services every Sunday at the church where she was an assistant minister (St Paul's, Westdale), for some three years before his death; & she had gotten to know him even better when he was first hospitalized with cancer; "He was such a lovely man, so kind, so generous, so brave, & humble - he never talked about his heroism in the war; other people told me about that"; & when he knew he was dying, he had asked her to conduct the funeral service (he who had railed against women in any professions, who could never have accepted women as priests, who tormented his wife to death!). Well, the telephone call came during a crisis involving my Ministry, which gave me a convenient excuse; but I don't think I would have gone anyway; I asked her to give him my regards etcetera. Then she telephoned again, a week or so later, to let me know about the funeral. Why did I go to it? But I did. The political crisis was over. So I had myself driven to the church, which I remembered seeing occasionally in my youth, and I sat in a pew near the back, next to a window illustrating the Epiphany. It was a full military ceremony; with veterans in uniform who formed a guard of honor for the coffin afterwards, as it was processed to the hearse. The young priest (very pretty in her white robe & black stole) eulogized him; he was not just one of Canada's War Heroes, he was a loving & lovable man; she had not known him long but she knew she would miss him deeply, though not as deeply as those who had known him longer & more intimately. Afterwards, before we set off for the cemetery, behind the hearse, I spoke to her very briefly, thanked her for what she had done for him in his last days & asked how I could contribute to the church in appreciation. "Oh, he was so proud of you, I'm glad you could come, it's such a pleasure to meet you" she said. "He was always talking about you, how successful you were in everything you ever did, how you were so important now in the Government, always so busy." "It's such a pity that you didn't know his wife." That's what I should have said. It might have saved me from the cold fury that attacked me, enveloped me; which is the most vivid memory I have of the service at my Father's grave-side; of course, there were the veterans, the priest, a bugler playing the Last Post, clods dropped on the coffin as it sank, & no doubt golden leaves floating down from the gallery of trees on a lovely sun-warmed Fall day? - but it is the sheer force of the fury shaking me, as I stood there, that I recalled now, as I stood again where I had stood those years before. You see, he had escaped the perdition that was the only just & rightful consequence of the suffering he had wreaked on his wife & son - escaped it, with the aid of this ignorant sentimental young female priest, & I could not accept that. All the way back to Queens Park I writhed in the plush back seat of my chauffered limousine. Even now, I writhe at the injustice of it. I wish I could say that, as I stood there again, a few days ago, gazing down at the grey army of gravestones (so many more than there had been then; now his one, then in company with some twenty-five others, was in the front row of about five hundred) half-submerged by the snow's thick expanse, I felt quite differently. I didn't. But when I made my way circuitously down to the graves' level, & crunched slowly to confront his grave ("James Edward McIsaac / Flying Officer / R.C.A.F. / October 31, 1986 / Age 73") I found that I was able to close my eyes & in my darkness pray for all of us. Is that a start?

Driving home, I turned on the radio; CBC. It was just before 10; Bach's "Air on a G String", arranged for the cello, sober & warmly solid (I have always enjoyed Bach more than any other composer); then Gordon Lightfoot, "Where the long river flows"; both so beautiful, & somehow so apt; I wept. When I reached home, I went straight to bed, feeling exhausted; & rose only when, late in the afternoon, my stomach demanded sustenance.

That evening, restless, I decided to go for another walk; this time along the new Desjardins Trail running from Princess Point, & beside the old Desjardins Canal's exit into the Lake, under the very bridge I had crossed twice that morning (the trail then runs on beside the railway-line towards the new Harborfront development (I had read about this trail some months earlier, in the *Spectator*); but I didn't go further than the lookout which gave a wide view of Stelco & Dofasco, across the Bay, & again the two low chimneys were belching their flame. As I walked back, I stopped to read a plaque commemorating the "Desjardins Canal Disaster"of Thursday 12 March 1857 when a train from Toronto "crashed through the wooden trestle, plunging sixty feet (twenty metres) into the frozen canal below"; fifty-nine of the ninety passengers aboard were killed; & "For many years after, this accident ranked as the worst in Canadian Railway history". As I looked up at the same great pillared stone supports (now upholding a steel railway-bridge), & heard the faint cries of frightened or hurt or dying people carried to me on the chilly breeze, I thought how appropriate it was that I should end my travels, this day, in the company of the dead; & then return to my silent, empty home feeling that they were happier than I am (until I join them).

8 MY QUEST: DAY TWO, SATURDAY 20 JANUARY 2001

Will you be surprised that I went back the next day? Doing that is very Me, I'm afraid. I needed to get the experience into a final order; to revisit it, to revise it - I guess that is part of the explanation; but it was also, by 9:20, when I stood again looking down on my Father's grave, a brilliantly sunny day as well as a bitterly cold one; the snow had frozen solid during the night (I think the temperature was predicted to go down to about -20), and was reflecting the rare sunlight fiercely. This time I felt neutral, mercifully bereft of any deep emotion; as if, in spite or because of my deep dreamless sleep, I was too weary to stay angry; as if I was at last ready to seek some resolution; to bury him, & with him my anger at what he did to us. Who knows, I may yet be able to move beyond that & try to forgive him; but for the moment neutrality is enough, isn't it? I can't manage more than that. Then I went on to Elaine's tree; stumbling on the hard ridges formed by the footsteps of those who had walked ahead of me. Again I sat on the bench below the tree; relaxing into the sun's sharp, distant warmth. My mind filled with memories of Elaine; I smiled at one - TT yanked at his lead just as she was clambering gingerly down a snowy slope, so she lost her footing & whirled inelegantly down to where I was standing ready to photograph her (she made me tear up that one!); & then memories of Margaret, & even of my Mother, came too; a calming procession. I felt happy, at ease.

(I am writing now on Saturday 27 January (soon to be Sunday 28 January). It is 11:50 p.m. Anne has just dropped me off after our night at the opera! Tchaikovsky's *Eugene Onegin*; a fine production by Opera Hamilton, meticulously directed, well sung, convincingly acted, at Hamilton Place. I went to it at Anne's invitation. Let me backtrack to explain that she & I did indeed lunch together a few days earlier; she took me to a simple quiet restaurant, &, as soon as we had ordered our meals, launched into a long disquisition about the resolution of her marital problem. My advice was no longer needed! She had tackled James about his late-comings, & it turned out that he had been meeting, not an old flame in a cheap hotel bedroom, but an old *friend* of his (school-friend, I think she said), one Brian Harrison (a lawyer); he had been trying to help this man save *his* marriage, which (this becomes almost incredible, a shaggy dog story!) was being undermined because, his wife similarly suspecting assignations with a woman, *he* has been trying to help a friend (known to James too) who is in prison! All this took some time to narrate, as you might imagine; but the result of the episode was clearly satisfactory to Anne. I was tempted to suggest (based on memories of my own career of marital deception) that she suspend her belief for a while longer & enquire further before exonerating James; but I didn't (& anyway he seems too grey to be doing anything not strictly legal & moral). I was happy to feel happy that *she* was happy, and to contribute occasional "Really?"s. At the end of the meal she leaned forward over her empty plate, looked deeply into my eyes & said "Daddy, I have enjoyed being with you so much, let's do it again, soon? Your advice is so important to me" (what advice?) & - "Oh, you know, I've just remembered to tell you that I have a spare ticket for the opera on Saturday night, James can't come, so annoying, he's got to see a client in Toronto, he can't possibly put it off, but I know how you love music" (do I?) & so - "I'll pick you up at about seven, then we'll have time for a drink before it starts" & before I could open my mouth she was briskly up, scraping her chair. As I said, she is rather forceful - or am I just getting old & doddery?

Anyway - the opera. And I did enjoy it; indeed, I was, unexpectedly, moved & even enraptured by it. I hadn't been in Hamilton Place since the last time Elaine & I went to a concert of the old Hamilton Philharmonic (oh, is that why I accepted Anne's invitation without demur? - *Elaine* was the one who loved music, Anne; I just followed her); but I always felt at home there; seated near the front of the highest of those soaring balconies, gazing, while the orchestra tuned up, at a warm harmony of rough grey cement, smooth brown wood & voluptuously red curtains & carpets; a fine space to fill with music. Tonight it was filled with the melodious pain of Eugene, Tatyana, Olga (silly Olga!) & Lensky. Before the curtain rose, a sepulchral voice informed us that the two principals were "indisposed" - the audience responded with a collective moan of disappointment - "but they have agreed to perform nevertheless." Somehow that deepened the experience for all of us; we were grateful not to be sent away into the chilly night, or fobbed off with understudies (but perhaps there weren't any!) - & surely our knowing the two stars were struggling, were hurt, deepened their performance & our response? I won't give a review (I'm not qualified); merely say that it was one of those theatrical experiences one should remember with joy & gratitude; & I do.

But I spoilt the occasion on the way home, sadly; I had even been turning over in my mind inviting Anne in for a coffee, but by the time we reached Ancaster we were so angry that even perfunctory farewells were an effort. In summary: I commented appreciatively on the opera's paradoxically anti-romantic romanticism ("Habit is a gift from Heaven as a substitute for happiness"!), its remarkable success in shifting the genre away from extravagant exaggeration and cliche (*Aida!)* into intimate domesticity (a heroine who sits around *reading*!); murmurs of apparent assent from Anne (probably beginning to trust my sanity?); but then, alas, I went on to say how little sympathy I felt for Tatyana & especially Olga (the first because, knowing she loved Onegin, she stayed masochistically with her old Prince; the second for her culpable girlish irresponsibility) - "So you blame them for the whole tragic outcome," flared Anne; "for poor Lensky's death, for poor poor Onegin's isolation - blaming the women for the men's suffering rather than their own arrogance and stupidity, their egotistic self-absorption - they *deserved* what they got, of course they did, it was Tatyana and Olga who were the victims, they never had a chance with those two men, why do you always do this, Daddy, why do you always automatically assume that women are the cause of any unhappiness, anything that goes wrong, can't you *see* how prejudiced - You never had any time for your children, for any of us, just because we are female, you can hardly bear to acknowledge us! And look what you did to Mummy, how you hurt her, how you just walked out on us, & she never says a word against you to us, she always says you are our father & that you do love us - well do you, *do you*, I don't think so, Daddy, I think you - " Well, you get the gist. She was weeping by now & beginning to drive so erratically that I was really concerned we'd have a collision or she'd lose control (she was driving too fast up the hill, too, paying no attention to the perils of snow & ice) & slide us off the road into a ditch. So when we reached my house, & she stopped the car & sat clutching the steering-wheel, breathing thickly, & dabbing at her eyes with a tissue, I silently gave her my clean handkerchief. After a few minutes she said a blubbery "Sorry, I guess Tchaikovsky got to me, I was always a fool for the *Pathetique* - sorry, I shouldn't have said those things. Good night, Daddy." What did I say? I was embarrassed, I think. "Don't worry about the handkerchief, Anne. I've got a drawerfull of them, I'll never use them all now. Please drive home carefully. Please. Thank you for taking me to the opera." I looked at her dusky profile. Yes, I should have leaned across & kissed her; yes; but I didn't.

9   MY QUEST: DAY THREE, SUNDAY 21 JANUARY 2001
Strange: after writing the passage above, I went to bed, after 1 a.m.

today (28 January), expecting to lie awake hour after hour, gazing into the darkness out of my turmoil of tangled emotions; but I didn't; I slept deeply for six hours, then woke up knowing exactly what I would do today: the same as I did last week (& have still to describe for you), on the final day of my little Experiment: attend the 10:30 communion service at St Paul's Anglican Church, Westdale.

Oh, but never never do the same thing twice! I am a slow learner. This time (Epiphany 3) the Rector was using the service as an Awards Ceremony, naming member after member of the congregation who had given exemplary service (in his very humble opinion) during the past year; this as a prelude to the annual Vestry Meeting, due to be staged after the service (of course I didn't stay for it); there was a definite feeling of unease around me, even abrasion; some not thanked sufficiently or annoyed about others undeservedly thanked, some of the unthanked hurt? (there certainly were some; as the Rector himself indicated during the post-service Notices, aplogizing for one notable omission). The whole "sermon" was an unfortunate parody, I thought, of one of the day's Lessons, in which eponymous Paul himself (Corinthians 1) bungles his way through a simple analogy of the Church to a human body - which, composed of many members, mutually interdependent (so far so good; oh but -), some members are less *respectable* than others, & some even need to be *clothed* (i.e., concealed)! - the penis being one of these, wouldn't you say? - can't let our God-created organs of generation hang out, in full view, can we?); I may have been responding rather negatively; but, really, Paul has done much damage to Christians & others, & continues to do so; not only in his patent distaste for sexuality, but in encouraging evasive, dishonest discourse. Anyway, I came home immediately, discontented; & don't think I will return to my Father's church; I had sat again (for the third time, in fact) in the same pew, left-back, beside the stained-glass Epiphany; but, as on the first occasion, my Father's funeral, there was no epiphany for me this morning.

The communion service last Sunday (21 January) was, however, a very different experience. Increasingly, undeniably, during that period in that church, I felt spiritually fulfilled; yes, ecstatic. All the lessons, & the psalm, spoke positively to me: "your land shall no more be termed Desolate" (Isaiah); "How priceless is your love, O God! - you give them drink from the river of your delights" (Psalm 36); "concerning spiritual gifts, brothers & sisters ... there are varieties of gifts, but the same Spirit" (Corinthians 1); the miracle at the wedding in Cana of Galilee, water into wine (John 2). The sermon (by a visiting priest) was witty

& lively, with interesting contextual information about Hebrew weddings (did you know that Jesus & his disciples were, or should have been, embarrassed at arriving without their potluck contributions, so that the Miracle may have been more to assuage his Mother's embarrassment than to extend the jollity?); the music was eclectic in what struck me as a quintessentially Anglican mixture of traditional hymns, Taize chants, & bouncy contemporary spirituals; & the congregation, too, seemed diverse, with family groups, students, elderly couples, & many more children than aged ladies (which was not what I had expected in this age of declining religious attendance!). I found that I was enjoying myself! The final hymn was so jauntily rhythmic that half the congregation were clapping & swaying (in an Anglican church!). I felt I was surrounded by potential friends. Afterwards, in the Coffee Hour downstairs in the Hall, several people introduced themselves & chatted with me. I was careful not to give my name, & nobody seemed to recognize me (so short is the fame of a provincial politician!); one elderly gentleman had so obvious a military bearing that I thought, for a moment, of asking him whether he remembered my Father. But all this was last week. I went home wrapped in radiant warmth, urging myself to return next Sunday; but that, as I have shown, was a mistake - I should have recognized that the earlier experience was exceptional, its joy in part stemming from my three-day quest; that in fact it was the climax of my quest! But, like any climax, any orgasm, was it a momentary rapture whose intensity is merely a preparation for the next? By going back today, didn't I imply that? Rather than receiving it as something precious, unrepeatable? Could it have been - last Sunday - an epiphany? As I sat in the Church beside that stained-glass representation of the Epiphany & rejoiced in my presence there, in that congregation at that moment - yes, I think some spiritual force was penetrating me, warming me; it felt like that. The dead, the living. So close!

I slept deeply & calmly that night. But even by the next morning, I knew it was over, fading, and later I knew it was gone, dead. Do *you* think it was an epiphany, Madam my Therapist? Do you think that on my three-day quest I moved forward at all? Or was it all self-deception? You have all the evidence I am able to provide, right here. I await your diagnosis.

(Today, Sunday 28 January, I discovered - when, as usual, I turned on the radio for morning company - is the centenary of Verdi's death, & "Choral Concert" was broadcasting live, from Milan, where he died, a performance of his *Requiem*; which Elaine loved deeply. I listened to it while dressing & then consuming my coffee & toast, & felt sustained by both Elaine's & the Great Man's spirits (a music master at school, Italian by descent, once played excerpts from Verdi operas while narrating, with justified adulation, the heroic life of his musical & national hero - "Victor Emmanuel Re D'Italia" I hear him pronouncing reverentially). Disappointed that the church service hadn't justified this noble prelude, I looked through Elaine's little collection of CDs this afternoon, but found no Verdi at all (I wonder what happened to those CDs); instead I put on what I remembered finding her listening to, in the few days after she was diagnosed with cancer & before she had to go into the hospital: the final section ("Der Abshied", "The Farewell") of Mahler's *Song of the Earth*. The mezzo-soprano's voice elided with Elaine's speaking voice (their similarly warm, deep timbre?) & as I followed the English translation (provided in the CD's booklet) it seemed as if Elaine was communicating with me - "All longing has turned to dreaming.... I stand here waiting for my friend, I wait to say my final farewell.... Where am I going?... I am seeking rest for my lonely heart.... Everywhere, the lovely earth blooms in spring ... Everywhere, forever, horizons are blue & bright!" Forever, forever - seven times repeated, in yearning ecstasy, "Ewig, Ewig, Ewig", sinking, sinking, sinking, until the final farewell meets & melds with eternal silence. My words cannot begin to match that glory of music; but can they tell you that, here, then, this afternoon - a week after my Quest, my Experiment, ended - listening to Mahler & hearing Elaine, I did reach an apotheosis of sorts? One even more intense than during last Sunday's communion service, an epiphany.)

10 CONCLUSION: PAST, PRESENT, FUTURE

My future! Why did I set this impossible topic. My fetish for planning, organizing, controlling. But I have already failed to fulfil my task, which seemed so simple and feasible; like any planned and considered business endeavour; perhaps one difference is that, as CEO of the large company that began so small and expanded & became a major employer in this city, I would receive, discuss, gather opinion, then come to a decision after careful, rational meetings of the Board (I encouraged dissent but almost always got my own way, which proved to be the best way - I had business acumen, & found that few others had it), & then implement it by allocating tasks to others & supervising them methodically, stringently (I tolerated no excuses, no poor performance; my staff knew that they either performed or were dismissed). But now I am on my own; no delegating! And I tire so easily, needing restful periods, even sleeps, during the day; & always with the bane of depression, that muffling darkness that can fall so suddenly and completely on one; the fear of it is itself inhibiting! Excuses, excuses! (Which I would never have accepted from any employee? How many did I dismiss out of hand; not even considering whether they might be suffering from depression? Unfair? No; as a businessman you have the profitability & welfare of a multitude to ensure; you are responsible; any individual who does not contribute as required must go, for the greater good. That I believe, Madam, implicitly. For the good of society as a whole, a defective individual, a bad workman spreading damaging habits, must be sacrificed; the alternative is to allow a creeping disease to sap vitality & eventually eviscerate all that is valuable in the society. Perhaps you do not agree? That was the argument underlying my opposition to any apparent endorsement or toleration of unmarried mothers: a debilitating social disease must be eradicated with every weapon available short of the ultimate (I do not believe in war to end war, a dishonest & distasteful paradox). (But my bleeding-heart colleagues, so principled until public-opinion surveys indicated that the Government would lose the next election if my proposals were endorsed - nothing like a coming election to bring the mice scurrying out to protect their cheese; how I despised them, those lily-livered, good-time, so-called colleagues; it was a relief to remove myself from their stench.)

This is my Conclusion? Of course it is not what I thought I was going to write! - but it will stand here until I can come back & replace it with an optimistic apolitical meditation full of my undoubted charm & intelligence, & garnished with simulated political correctness."My Rosy Future"! "The Happy Future I Deserve"! Perhaps, deep down (I am guessing your thoughts while reading this), I do not expect to have a rosy future, do not think I deserve one. Is that your diagnosis?

No, there is more to say. I had a fall, lost my footing on the ice while walking two days ago, in the evening; struck my head against a tree; and today I have a black eye! (Actually I feel quite proud of it: a romantic mystery!) (So I will continue these meditations on my life (now that I have decided to ignore my initial self-set deadline) in a suitably chastened state, Madam my Therapist.)

11 APPENDIX
I pondered hard before continuing beyond my planned ten items (one per day). Life is defeating me; again, again. My weariness; my sleeplessness; the growing fear that I am sinking towards another period of Depression. (Fragments, fragments! It is not your influence alone, Madam; I exonerate you; the sentence-fragment is my right-

ful style, whatever the grammarians legislate; I am become a Man of Fragments; perhaps always was; I am shedding myself, fragment by fragment; who will rescue me - will you, Madam? Oh keep away from the dead & the dying & the living dead! The air is filling with death, I breathe it, I breathe it. In India they are frantically digging up thousands of rotting corpses entombed by the earthquake; each one a human being, an individual personality, just hours ago; how can the brain endure this, how can any of us chatter on? - habit, habit.)

Dear God, dear God; please not! Preserve me, if only for a week, a day, from my next Darkness! But having insulted Him so often (in this report as on other occasions), I have certainly invited his Demons to punish me; again, again. (Is my Black Eye a symbol of God's wrath, haha?)

11   APPENDIX 2

Tuesday 30 January. (A dismal, dismal day. And dangerous. Fog, freezing rain, icy roads - accidents and no doubt deaths as people drive to work. The worst sort of Ontario winter day. Depressing even if you are not depressed! I went out for some exercise; walked in Ancaster, along the main street: the snowbanks melting into filthy slush as our great thaw continues; water wherever one trod, grey polluted shoe-destroying water, unable to gurgle down drains still blocked by ice and snow. But I am here; my word-machine hums in expectation, my screen glows invitingly. But what shall I write? What have I to communicate today, now?)

(My black eye is become very emphatic!)

I have not told you much about my actual political career, have I? Look me up in *Canadian Who's Who*. Not, however, a career of great moment: I merely contributed to a Government that claimed to be dedicated to renewed fiscal and personal responsibility (& a rational loathing for the wasteful sentimentalities of socialism), & all the other goodies every government promises, truth & openness & integrity & compassion, etcetera, etcetera. "Political correctness" indeed! But, as I think I said above, my brand of integrity etcetera rapidly offended my watchfully, jealously idle colleagues, more interested in retaining their ill-gotten positions, which they thought were at risk in an election that (because, you may not remember, it was a coalition government) avoided debating policy or advocating for substantial & necessary change. And then, after winning that election, our revered Premier insisted on trying to Save The Country, taking us all into the quicksand of Meech Lake, forgetting what we'd been elected for - I saw what was going to

come, the fate of being swept, with that jerry-built attempt to appease
Quebec nationalism, over the edge & into deserved oblivion. So I was
glad I had every respectable reason to get out when I did. I'd lost faith
in the party, its leaders, and my colleagues. Most of them, I soon ob-
served, did "bugger-all" anyway (an inelegant term of my Father's, as in
"You'll do bugger-all when you grow up, you cowardly little shit!"; well,
Daddy, you were wrong; or partly wrong; I may not be a Canadian War
Hero, or one of Canada's richest businesmen & best-known politicians,
but I didn't try to fuck-up my wife & child - & then take refuge in the
ignorant mercies of the Anglican Church!).

I feel tense today: am I treading close to the edge of the precipice
again?

("Blind mouths!" Do you know that famous expletive, Madam
Therapist? Yes, from one of Milton's Sonnets - we studied it at high-
school; I can't remember the rest of it, but that phrase was in my mind
when I awoke this morning. Why? What defunct dream spawned it?
Or did God put it there? Milton was excoriating those who betrayed
the Word, if I remember rightly; but I don't doubt that whoever put the
phrase in my mind - God or myself - was excoriating Me. My verbose
disorganized stupidity - as displayed so definitively in this puerile Report. Once (you will hardly believe this now) I prided myself on being
precise, succinct; would have sent back to its perpetrator a document
like this one, marked with my curt command "Review, revise, reduce!"
But that was then, & I am not what I was. I think I have become a fool-
ish, fond old man. (I wish you could have met me in my prime, Madam
my Therapist! But that is my vanity talking. As, no doubt, it has done
through all these many pages. Word after word after word. A Waste
Land of words. Vain, yes, but my Pride is long gone, wasted away (for
those who can see, who care to see, or are paid to see). (I cannot even
control my punctuation now; whole sentences, expire in dark forests
of parentheses.) I think I need your help, Madam; I beg it of you. I too
am waiting for Godot. My life is a Hole. My life is a Hole. Please help
me if you can.)

12 APPENDIX 3

Closure! This day (Wed 31 January), weather-wise, is a slight improvement on yesterday. The thaw continues; but snow is predicted to
return, &, I think I heard, so are colder, below-freezing temperatures;
winter is far from over; no point in thinking about spring yet (one
of the supermarket cashiers on Monday cheerfully asseverated that
"Spring is almost here!" - can female intuition be more fallible?) Also,

I am to meet you, Madam my Therapist, in just over three hours (at 10 a.m.). I shall hand this report to you then, as printed by my little printer (beginning at 8:30 so I have time to staple it & seal it in the envelope I have already addressed to you); but I am ashamed of its inadequacies; it is a mess, let me say that honestly, manfully; disordered rather than orderly; & I apologize for that. I simply have not had the time or (perhaps more importantly) the energy to reconsider & revise, as I planned & expected to do (although I did manage intermittent revision). It is much too long! I know, I know. I thought of abandoning it as a bad job (which it undoubtedly is); but again, I promised, I undertook, I must deliver. Who was it said "If a thing is worth doing, it is worth doing badly"? Well, here it is, my bad job. By the time you read this (& there's always the chance that you won't!), you & I will have met, & formed at least an initial opinion about each other, & about the likelihood or unlikelihood of a good professional relationship. (My "black eye" has paled slightly, but the bruise is still a narrow smudge underneath my right eye. You will of course notice it; but how will you react? Will you pretend not to see it, or ask me directly what happened? You see, I will be assessing you as you will be assessing me!)

Did I mention that my daughter Anne has invited me (if "invited" is the right word; more like another command; I remember how her half-sisters used to call her "Bossy Boots") to a "family gathering" next Sunday? She did so last Sunday afternoon, in a telephone call following our angry parting in the wake of *Eugene Onegin* the previous night; said she'd called to apologize for what she'd said to me, & hoped that I would forgive her. Well, Madam my Therapist, I am not totally beyond human feeling, & knowing her haughty nature (so very like mine) I knew what that apology would have cost her, so I said No, it had not been her fault; it had been mine; that it had been a glorious evening & I would never forget it & I was truly grateful & had enjoyed her company (even to me, it sounded like some imposter talking; unconvincing, stiff, formal). I almost added "And I love you" but didn't, couldn't (that would have gone too far - & I don't know whether it's true!). She just said "Oh Daddy" & then, after a pause, "Look, I'm having all the family over next Sunday for dinner, we try to have a family gathering every month, could you come, we'd love you to come, James will come & pick you up?" So I found myself, again, meekly saying Yes (though insisting that I could & would drive myself over). But of course I may change my mind. "Family gathering" implies, no doubt, two ex-wives exchanging collusive glances, a phalanx of three daughters (I doubt if Tracy would come from Kingston for the occasion), two mumbling husbands trying to think of what to say to an old dotard they barely recognize, the five grandchildren mutedly milling about & being ordered to say Hi Nicely to Granddad. And what have I to say to any of them? What do they mean to me? What do they have to do with me?

(I had been wondering how to complete this verbose, disorganized, & all-too-inadequate report. But contingency has, as always, come to my aid. Always trust Contingency! The Word of God! His way of keeping us in order! On the CBC radio news, which so often introduces me to the new day & its repetitive agonies: Lockerbie, a verdict, so many years after that disaster (how many? - I missed that; ten?); one parent of a victim, leader of the group, fainted in court (an old man, he must be; his life ruined by an event that had nothing to do with him, except that his daughter happened to be aboard that plane that night); others are already demanding a public enquiry in England, to find Closure (closure! - how does one close off such pain & loss, how does one cauterize one's memories, one's being?). But what most interested me was the verdict itself: one defendant was found guilty, one was not found guilty. I thought immediately of the Thieves on the Cross, Beckett's *Waiting for Godot*, in a production of which I acted during my final year at college (I was Lucky! - learning all that gibberish must be having a late effect on me here, though one might say that it stimulated me to became Pozzo thereafter, lashing my slaves into remunerative productivity!); I thought then, & still do, that Beckett's play is a scarifyingly, profoundly truthful exposition of the Nature of Human Existence. Listen: "There were two thieves. One was saved. One was condemned." (That doesn't sound quite right; but close enough; & - why don't we have a Theology of Dualism? - after all, our world cannot be comprehended except as pervasively dualistic, cold defining hot, good evil, God Satan, & so on & so on.) Continuing this day's dose of duality, there was another notable item in the CBC news: An international incident in Ottawa; two members of the Russian Embassy staff have claimed diplomatic immunity & have been sent back to their decaying homeland after causing, while drunk-driving after a party, two serious accidents; in one, nobody is killed; in the other, two women are struck; one of the two is killed, the other not, merely badly injured & in hospital. But what is any of this to do with me, today, any day, personally, impersonally? It is the scientific underpinning that fascinates me. Is it always there? Blatant this morning; but doesn't every moment of our lives contain it: plus, minus; the road taken, the road not taken? And so I do come back to myself, after all!

(I telephoned the estate-agent a short while ago, and told him that

I had decided, for the moment, not to sell my house; but perhaps in Spring - . Trivial or momentous decision?)

I am a Man of Fragments (see above). (The Man of Order has disintegrated into the Man of Fragments; or was he always so, a collocation of fragments under his black suit & natty tie?) You are Our Lady of Compassion, of Healing, of Miracles. Can you put me together again? Where my Head & Heart should be, Madam my Therapist, I am a Hole. It's not a case of "Is there a hole in your life?" - my Life *is* a Hole? (Oh, that agonizing pun again! I repeat myself, I repeat myself. Truly it is time to go; time to search for Closure, a way of ending this outpouring of words, words, words.)

By the way, my doctor is sending me for further tests. Urgently. The result of the AP test (is that what it's called? - blood-test for prostate cancer) that they administered before Christmas is not, it appears, *quite* as hoped; in fact, falls firmly into the negative; gently, encouragingly, "We need to be sure" etcetera, with smiles and jokes; I told him that his patients must die laughing, and he looked at me and said "They die anyway". Prostate cancer! Another of God's little jokes; surely heart disease or brain cancer would make a more appropriate exit for me! But then I guess I kept that little guy hard at work most of my life, and finally he's had enough of all that squeezing and squirting, and now he's outta here, poor little guy, and determined to take me with him. (Perhaps he thinks I'll need persuading? If I believed that I would be reunited with Elaine, for all eternity, at the moment of our first mutual orgasm -

But I must end, I must stop. I can't stop. I *must* stop. I *will* stop. Time, Gentleman, please. Time to go.

Signed:

Will I end my days in this my present house in Ancaster or its replacement (I am thinking of selling it & purchasing a townhouse)? I think so, but I have also learned some lessons in the past five years about the unpredictability & insecurity of life; so, in writing this document for you, I was also reassuring myself that I am of sound mind & healthily sanguine temperament. I should warn you (if this fact is not stressed in your predecessor's comments & observations, in the file which I trust he passed on to you; & in this document) that I am precise & meticulous in all I do (or almost all); direct & I hope clear in all I say or write; & do not welcome attempts to redirect my life, at my somewhat advanced age. I will now

TEN
Last Things

THIS FOR MISTER PETER ABBOT
PRIVATE! MY PRISON DIARY?!!!
Sunday Jan 14th, 2001
My Freind, I dont know where to start. Its cold in here still! Hard
to write, my fingers are stiff. You can see that, you know my writing
is bettr! I got the furnase going, an the wood-stove, there was wood
in here and paper & matches. I knew there wd be. I remember from
when I was here with you!!? So, easy to start a fire. An I switchd on the
hydro too, but I wont put on the lights in the big room sos nobody will
take notice. Only the light in the bedroom, with the cutains closed Im
sitting here now. Guess they might see the smoke, but I dont think so
- too far away, your nearest nighbor, and all the trees. Its funny I am
here here in your cotage and you don't evn know! Well, you know now!
when you reading this!?! But right now while I'm writng this you don't
know an when you do know, will be aftr I am gone. Unless you come
here sudenly!!?? Well, gradualy getting warmer in here now. I made
some tea for myself! You lagh at that!! you know I NEVR drink tea!??
But lots of teabags in that litle tin can with Fathr Chrstms on it. An I
got food bread & cans of tuna-fish & jiuce & water & all, an some cans
of stuff here. Thanks!?! Tomorow Ill bring in more wood, know you got
lots in the shed. So, here I am. Wish you wer here with me now!

Today it is a gray day. Like ysterday. Got here in the midle of last
nigt an I just lay down on yr bed with all my cloths on an I put all the
blnkts on me from all the beds! Then I got warm slowly. On friday

when I came out of jail it was gray at first also. Nancy was there & Sam, Eric was at school. They went with me in the taxi straght to the hospital, Nancy said we must do that an I wantd to do that & you know its free too, the taxi, sos you can get home or wherevr, but it was to late. It was to late. My Mum wasnt evn there any more. They said she died last night. Sudden, they said it was anothr stroke took her and how she dint suffr, all those lies they tell. I cried, I wanted to see her once evn dead, just wanted to see her an Say goodby. But they said shes gone, her body gone to the undertakr & they wd ask him to call us an tell us about the funral & when it wd be. And I ws angry!? Why dint they let me come out in time why dint they? So we went home.You know, the apartmnt were you visitd Nancy once an the kids - that time when I ws still inside. So then I went to sleep. I slept fr 3 hrs. I was tired!!!

I just turned yr radio on! & out comes ABBA! "Knowing me knowing you there's nothing we can do???" - next I guess it'll be "Money, money, money"!!! Shitty words, crappy singn! Not MY CUP OF TEA!! Hey, I'm joking! Yes, Mistr Abbot, My Lord an Master, I know you don't talk like that??? But I bet you do like ABBA! Like you do like the Beatles!!? Oldmens trash!!! I wish I had some of my cd's that got stoln here, Rolin Stones, the Who, & all. I just looked thro the cd's you got here. All calsical trash of course!!!! But I rembr you playd me this one, Four Last Songs, Richard Strauss, you realy likd it you said so Ill put it on latr. Aftr dinnr!!! An Ill smoke a litle weed like we did togethr, I cdnt belive you nevr had it before, you are same age as the Beatles OLD MAN, & THEY all smokd up! That ws a good time, my good man! we hanged out togethr, you startd laghing and cdnt stop you talkng bullshit, so was I, I always rembr tht day. COOL!?! You frgoten??? Nancy said she dint have any joints an she stopd smoking up while I was inside No more drugs nevr But she lied an when she out for Eric, walkng home with him from school, I fnd weed and hash and coke & all under the bed but I only took some weed.

That night we talked & talked!!! Its like Im talkng to you NOW! I wondr wher you ar, can you hear me, course not, I wish you wer here and we cd smoke up togethr! Hang out togethr!!It's gettn dark now. Snow everywher, deep snow up here, much deeper hey thn in Westdale! An I ben out fr a walk!!! Suprise!? Also I got lots of wood in frm yr shed so tonight Ill be warm in here and also I found yr cloths all old ones of course!!! MR FASHION Sweaters & yr old coats Thanks!!?

My Freind. You suprisd that I came here? Dint know where to go. Just startd drivng & drivng & I was going north, I dint evn think at frst but then Im goin north on the 6 and I thoght yes I'll go to My Frend's cotage its empty in winter cos he dosent go an Itl be easy to brake in. I notisd that when I was here with you that time.You need better lock on the back door!!!You are CARELESS, just like you said your mom said you are. CARELESS!! I just pusht hard with my shoulder, couple times, no problem! an I got the flashlight from the car. So here I am.

Remember how I promisd I wd write a Prison diary for you???? Well I startd one inside but then dint finish it, but you can get it, what I rote, its with my stuff in my bag in

No I forgot. Its gone. Everything is gone for me. An I will be gone soon to.

This is for you. Want to tell you all that hapenned. I was looking forwrt to seeing you again, My Freind. Now I wont. Never. Not evn aftr death, youll be in Heaven & Ill be in Hell. You know thats true!!! God punishs Evildors. Don't evn pray fr me wd be a waste of breath. I want to talk to you but I cant. Im looking at the phone & thinking I cd just pick it up & dial yr numbr and youd answr maybe but I cant. So I got to go on writng my diary insted. You know on friday night late I walked past yr house *twice*. Told Nancy I got to go out & walk. We been smoking up but I was tight, like tight all ovr, my head was achng. So I walkd an walkd, I walked to the hospital but I dint go in, so then I walk all round Westdale fr hours, past all those posh houses & it was cold my hands were aking & the sidewalks were a mess so I walk out on the rd & some cars blew there horns at me but I didnt care and they just went round & one guy yelld. The snowbanks was high, high as my waste an ther wer lots of Chrstms trees on top of the snowbanks wating fr t garbage and som Christmas lights still on the houses & trees flashing away. Yr Christmas tree was there lying on the snow but you were out, yr house was all dark! I remembr you said how you may go to yr sistr in Montreal fr New Years & spending time with yr Mother too but thoght youll be bck by now or you on some hotshot drugs case in TO just kiddng but I know you lawyrs!!! always making a few more million bucks!!? Calld you next day too when I woke up no answr. Only the porch light was on. So I went. And I got home and Nancy and the kids was asleep an I nocked on the window and she let me in and I went to sleep an I slept all next mrng. An when Im walking in Westdale I thought about how everyone had a good Christms & New Years maybe! but all gone now for anothr yr & my mom dead to an I won't be around fr nxt Chirstmas for sure. Hope you had a good one! Did you go to your Mom in Ottawa I wonder??? have a Happy New Years My Frieind! wherevr you are

You know what hapenned, it was in all the papers, and I heard it on

the radio to, while I was drivng up here. Looking fr me!!?! DANGER-
OUS an ARMD don't intrfear with him!!!?? I thought the guy might
notis me whn I stoped for gas, whn I went in to pay, but he was to busy
reading a book!!! Americn Sycho!! But I want to tell you about wht
hapennd myself so's you know it all the truth because you my Friend.
Sos you know I nvr meant to hurt hr, nvr ment to kill her, you know
I nevr wd. It was a acidnt. So Now I will writ this Diary & tell you
evrythng like in that prison diary I didnt finish but here it is, My Frend.
I hope you not laghing abt my spelling like you use to. I need you to
corect my spelling!!! like whn you typed out my poems when you came
in on Tues aftrnoons for the guys & we all talked togethr and abt our
poems.

You know I love you My Freind and I know you love me whervr you
are. That time here in this cotage, it was in the fall, 1999, hey, when we
smokd weed thats whn you said you wer maybe gay & I said I wasnt
gay an I hate gays, the Bible says it a sin you rembr how we talked abt
all that. It was true, what I said then but

<u>15 Jan 2001 Monday</u>
I cdnt finish last night didnt know wht to say stll dont but doesnt
matter any more anyways but I wanted to tell you that I do love you all
the same and I allways will love you. Abbot, you bn My Freind & I am
Your Freind for evr & evr amen!

Now I got to tell you what I did. But I been rembering tht time we
wer here togethr. Jst one time bt I remerd the way. It was Fall yr before
last. Septembr 1999. Like I see in the Second song of yr FOUR LAST
SONGS, I listend last night, calld "SEPTEMBER" did you know yr cd
has the words for them in that litle bk they put in with the cd? The
words she sings, its in german, but they have english words in there an
I read them all so now I know what she is singing. Its in September
like whn I was here with you an it says the garden is in mourning like
I am in mourning for my mom an for Nancy. An it says about the rain
and leaves droping and so on what sort of peotry is that!!! CRAP!!!
Garbage. Thats what I think.You want to argue??? Remembr how you
said my poems wer the REAL THING thats what you said??! So how
can this be real poetry??? Remember how you and all the guys laghed
& you said it was great, my one called "ALLEY CAT" about the gy in
that alley remember tht one??? You said it was great poetry. All the gys
laghing an you too & you said it must be great poetry it makes us all
lagh. And you said poems cd be abt anythng esp what really hapens to
you & evn if its sad or ugly makes you lagh makes you feel happy sort

of thats what poetry does Its the TRUTH But this poetry on yr cd is shitty, My Man! Dont make me lagh at all! Abt leaves droping!!??? But the music is good its differnt and its sad sort of sad.

Well today it was gray to. And foggy. Misty you wd say "misty"! Rember that poem you brought an we all discused it it was by Lenard Cohen, tht guy with the deep voice like yrs hes the one that sings IM YR MAN?! So, tht poem went "The mist leaves no scar on you and Nevr will

I dident mean to do it. My Freind. It was a accident. I came back it was cold & dark I taped on the window and she lets me in & I was hungry & she wnt give me money & I need to by food and stuff & she says O no Youll by booze & I say no I wont but still she sayin I know you will an I say No how can I with the Antabuse I wd be sick as a dog Id die and she said you dint take it I dint see you takin no pills and I say yes I did you were sleeping and then she Anyways wasnt her money it was McGregr's an then I know fr sure she been into drugs selling drugs while I been Inside she been selling weed & hash & smack an all for McGreger and then Eric comes in he been out playing with the other kids & he has his hockey stick so I grab it & I lose it & I say to Nancy give me the money for the last time & she says No I wont you cant have it I wont give it its for the childrn an then I hit her with it & she falls an just lays there looking at me & Eric comes running an he pushes me so I hit him to with it & he holds my leg so I hit him & his head bangs on the floor then I hit Nancy too shes trying to get up, I dont know what Im doing Im crazy crazy then I hear Sam in the bedroom and shes callng Mommy Mommy so then I run away shut the door and I hear somones coming down the stairs but Im gone. So Thats how it hapenned & thats the truth an I dint mean it. An then I dont know wher to go. An then I thought Ill go to Mcgreger I'll get money from him an I went I walk up to Ancaster I got there an

Tell you tomorow Tired now got to get to bed. I taken my medication you know Paxodil and all but only a few left now two days maybe. Now I got to get to bed Sleep.

But I met someone this afternoon a woman. I was walkn in the woods behind an Near the beaver-dam you showed me last time rember we saw one we watched it swiming and swiming. The snow melting thawing warmer today an raining an the trees all driping. Got my feet wet. The ski trails still hard where the skis been, slipery but everytime you step off it Im sinking deep. Yr boots!!! I found boots in the closet, big ones, I knew they wase yrs "YOU GOT FUCKIN BIG FEET MY MAN!!!" but I put on 3 prs socks so then they fittd me good enough & I was watching wher I walkin & I didn't hear her & then we met sudenly. We just stoped & looked she was skiing and said Hi and I said Hi an she smiles says Sking not good today but she just neded to be out get some exercise. She didnt act frightend at all. She goes You visiting here & I go Yes an she Oh were you come from an I say Owen Sound Im just going back I live there my cars bck therin the lane. Sos she wont tell nobody Im here. Sos if she tells the police they lookng fr me in Owen Sound!!?! an I say my names Eric I cdnt think eny other name fast an I say Guess I better make tracks I got to be back in Owen Sound an then I went an she went. Funy how she jst sudenly apeared like tht. So I come home here & open another one of the cans for dinner I got them from McGreger's place & juce & stuff & also I stoped on the way fr gas & I got more food with McGregers money!!

So. Now Ill put more wood in the wood-stove an go get some sleep. Wondrng where you are tonight. "Time to sleep Put out the light and then put out the light!!!" Shakespear rember how we read those speeches Inside & that was one. I remember now it was Othello. You said it was at the end. Goodnight, My Feind wherevr you are. Put out the light!!! The end!

On the radio it said Eric died not Nancy & abt "Nancy may live" injurys but may live but I think they got it wrong. I didnt hit Eric that hard.

Tues

Woke up I cdnt sleep last night I forgot my medicatn when I shd take it I was listning to the radio MY MUSIC!! hard rock & "HEAVY METEL" & all but I turnd it bck to CBC & I took medicatn late so I woke up & I was feeln tight I smoke up in the dark an listen to the music on the radio then I felt bettr & I went back to sleep but I woke up early ths mrng and the radio was on. an I hear on the news abt a big earthquake in San Selvadar I think it was, poor guys & abt two lttle guys here nr Cornwall, 16 yrs & 14 yrs they are brothrs & the oldst one was bullied at school & he wrote a story abt how he wd bomb the school!!? and they put him in jail!! & then they put his ltle brothr in jail too he was mad & he was bullied too & he wrote that he wd kill them all & they put him in jail too how cd they do that!?! You bettr go there & be there lawyr!! Maybe thats where you are I hope so. How can they do that it was a STORY he dident DO IT an they dont know the differnce they dnt know abt poetry & writing I HOPE YOU TELL THEM!! those poor litle guys in jail & theyll be fucked up there like I was drugs & stuff & like McGreger then theyll get out & do it & end up

like me maybe. And I heard abt whats his name Wallinburg I think He
saved jews in the war & they killd him too but wont say how He was
a HERO & they killd him too. Sombody shd write a bk abt him & abt
those litle guys in jail so they don't go on doing those shitty thngs to
people I hope you agree My Friend!!! So here I am talkin to you agan
& now I feel calm Its goin to be a good day I know it is I feel that An
its so quiet here I cant believe it when I woke up last night it was like
the silence was noisy I wanted to write a poem abt it how the silence
is noisy know what I mean? Also I heard yr music on the radio CBC
& it was great I was laying here & I realy enjoyd it are you suprised??
The guy said it was a symphny by don't know if thats spelt right I think
it was Sibaylis, numbr 2, and it was like I was going on a long jurney
in the snow thats what I thought and like fighting with monstrs and
wind blowing snow in yr face & its getting dark its night & monstrs
& a humungus storm and you slip off the path and you in the snow &
losing the way & you going to die right out there on yr own in the snow
& just freeeze an dont care any more just want to die but you dont &
then you walking and strugling and walking and then it was like calm
& you resting leaning on a tree in the woods an gettin yr breath then
you have to move on & the storm comes black and the wind but you
gettin there an the drums & trumpets loud! an you almost there & you
going to make it & the drums & trumpets & then you do MAKE IT
you get home you get home at last HOME!!! But Wallinburg didnt get
home. They killd him.

Now its later! & I been sitting in here & listening to music & I been
thinkng "THIS IS MY HOME!!!" You think I am crazy?? I am crazy.
All on my own here & this is HOME??? But I think my mom is here, &
you to. All three of us. You usd to ask me abt when I was a litle boy &
I dident want to talk abt it. Why because I had no father he went away
when I was a baby dint want me so I only had a home once. With my
mom befor she married. Then HE was there & HE hated me I wanted
to run away. But I was hapy before when it was my mom & me, an we
had a home it was in Kingston & a store underneath it was a great place
& she still loved me she gave me things hockeystick & skateboard &
all It was before she married & we came to Hamilton an then she had
other kids & she stopd loving me HE made her do it but she shdnt do
that I cried I cried & I still lovd her but no home I staid away HE beat
me up & I hated him I hated him I shdnt the Bible says its sinful but
I stll did. But I lovd her. I was happy when I was a litle kid it was my
ONLY HOME I nevr had another home. But I been thinking abt Im
happy here. I been sitting here & just thinking & thinking abt all my

life. Its my last day almst. I got to go tomorow. My medicatn finishd
soon & not much food & watr left & "THE END IS NY!!!!" But I am
happy today.This is HOME too. I was happy when we was here in Sept
1999 just you & me fr one day but it was HOME. Now I think my mom
is here & you are here with me!!! See CRAZY. Do you think I am crazy
Mr Abbot!!? Home number ONE I was a litle boy with my mom home
numbr 2 we was here you & me & home numbr THREE now I am here
on my onio but my mom & you here with me."CRAZY!"

Later. Afternoon nearly over. Flurries we had flurries like the radio
said & more toniht an its gettin real cold agn well below freezing -20?
I been out to bring in more wood for the woodstove & all the snow
laying around. I been sitting her most of day listning to music on the
radio & also yr cd "Four Last Songs" for the last time. Everything almst
for last time now. My last night here. My last home. I put the light on
here in the main room an I'm sitting on the sofa & I left the cutains
open. Nobody come for me I dont think they wll but if they want they
can Im waiting & Im ready but the news on CBC says the police still
looking for the car at the border & in the US an also lookin for Mc-
Greger. Some other guy was killed in Hamilton same day I rembr him
from Barton Street small guy skiny? he been out for three months from
Warkworth then hes stabed to death they think McGreger got something to do with it? Why he wasnt home?? Anyways, don't matter to
me now. I thoght they might find the car but they havent so that guys
cotage still empty!? But anybody can see me here now in the cotage I
don't care nomore. An I look out & the snow that was laying all around
changing color it was like blue & the clouds were pink & gray. Then I
put out the light to see how it wd look & then the snow had like a light
shining deep inside. Difernt it was like glowing. It was like everything
was outside & nothing inside like I was a gost An then I put on the light
a bit later & DIFERNT you cd hardly see the snow at all it was purple
& snowflakes falling softly & the windows reflecting everything inside
the room an it was like evrything outside was a gost now almost gone
into the darkness. An I thoght that was like me & us & Home??? Like
Im here but Im not here & Im changing all the time & like my mom
& you are here even tho I cant see you. & like all three of us are in the
light & in the dark to & different & the same I thoght abt the words
fr the third song its calld BEIM SCHLAFENGEHEN german GOING
TO SLEEP english an how it says "And the spirit unguarded longs to
soar on free wings, so that, in the magic circle of night, it may live
deeply, and a thousandfold" And I thoght Thats crappy poetry but Like
we ARE surounded by the magic circle of night, thats what I seen with

my eyes. And our spirits long to soar like it says on free wings & live deeply, and a thousandfold!!! The magic circle of night. "Thats POET-RY!?". But the music is great and I'm sleepy like it says too. Had some food some orange juice took my medicatin put wood in the woodstove ready to get into bed Sleep sleep sleep. Goodnight.

Radio still saying Eric dead not Nancy no no they got it wrong I dident hit him hard he cdnt die it was Nancy.

Wed 17th Janury 2001

My last day!! Its sunny then the clouds come then sunny agan. And its cold & latr flurries I think the radio said Slept good took medicatn smokd some weed & felt good & I slept good.

I been thinkng abt that car. Cd get it & drive away in it but where to. I nearly did that I startd to walk to that place the cotage where I left it the snow crunchy now frozen in the night then I thoght Maybe the owner has come back now why pay for yr driveway keep it clear if you staying away? Maybe hes looking at the car now thinking WOW whos car black MERC! why is it here in my garaje?? Maybe hes thinking just keep it I wd & tell nobody findings keepings my mom used to say that! but maybe hes calld the police maybe they are there wating for me So I didnt go Anyway I don't want it no more No more traveling "WE ARE RESTING FRM OUR TRAVELS NOW, IN THE QUIET COUNTRY-SIDE"!!!? I hope you resting My Freind. I know my mom is resting. Sun coming out. "O SPACIOUS, TRANQUIL PEACE" it says & We must not go astray in this solitude. You think that is Real Poetry?? Its differnt but like you say it makes me feel deep inside not laghing & not sad but its deep makes me feel good Like "TRANQUIL" I looked it up in yr dictinary here Calm Peaceful I hope Nancy and Eric & Sam "tranquil" & my mom & you Mistr ABBOT

So. Got to get ready. Got to tidy up yr place I messed it up a bit sorry. Wearing yr cloths & eating yr cans of tuna & soup!!!?

But I nevr told you abt McGreger remember I told you I went ther aftr I ran away I thoght people chasing me looking for me but its quite just cars going past it was getting dark. I got no money for the bus so I go on walking & walking up the hill to Ancaster & I get ther & I go to McGregers place I been ther before when I was out before He took me ther He said look me up when you out & Ill fix you up his hotshot lawyer got him off you remembr You said, if you got money like he has & contacts like he has you can by wht you want nevr mind whet the law says So Im in Ancastr & its dark its snowing hard He got a big posh place I go to the front door & lights shining out & I ring the bell & no

anser no sounds So I push the door its not evn locked & I go inside
& I shout McGreger Mcgreger its Derek you here me??? And funny,
its quiet, no anser no anser & I go into the kitchen & nobody nobody
& Im getting worried feels funy & I need to go hes not here & I seen
the black Merc outside & now I see a bunch of keys on the tabel in the
hall an som money so I get som food & juice from his refrigerter Im
hungry & then Im in the Merc & it starts like a bird & Im driving &
driving. So where is he whats he doing whys his front dor unlocked
& lights on But Im driving north Thats how it hapenned!!! And still
they don't know where McGreger is thats wht the CBC news says I
wondr where hes gone like in a big hurry Its like somebody came &
picked him up maybe & he hd no time they was in a hury??! Anyways
Im drivng & then I think abt yr cotage & I head for hear. Thats what
hapend, My Frend. & Wht a plesur to drive a MERC I nevr driven one
before like a bird real smooth it's a great car!!? When I get here cdnt
drive off the rd snow to high in the driveway so I go on & I see that old
guy yr friend whos driveway hs bn cleard & I drive up If hes there I say
oh sorry, mistake, but no lights an hes not there no car in his garaje so
I put McGregr's car in there & I carry stuff to the cotage thro the trees
& go back & get all the food & water & all & then Im set up!!?!

I been writing some poems for you TRASH I throwed it away trash
but how abt this one. Only a litle one!!?? Just for you. Abbott!!

"Goodby My Freind.
Getting dark, Mist & snow.
Time to leave, time to go.
The end My Freind, the end"

I got to go soon. When its elevn whn my watch says 11 PM. Snowing hard now. Im looking at the flakes jumpng up & down fightng &
kissng & messng abt in the darkness bt in the end they lay down on
top of each other & afetr that rest in peace they are "tranquil calm &
in peace".

So I tidied up the place. Did all my pissing & shitting outside under
the trees so no mess inside!! but I put things back. Sory abt breaking
the lock on the back door but it ws shit anyway You shd by a good
strong new one MISTER RICH BIGSHOT LAWYER!! then I wont
be able to get in nxt time Im passing by!!?! Ill put my filthy cloths &
yrs to that I bn wearing in a plastic bag mine smell but yrs are full of
HOLES don't you have no pride in yr apearanse!!!?? & Ill leav them
in the garbaje can outside.& Yr BIG BOOTS I left them in the corner

of the bedroom. I wont take any with me Im going to strip my cloths filthy anyways & I don't want yrs So naked!!! The way I came into this world & Ill go out of it naked to. So now I am finishing this diary My Freind. Lucky you left this writing paper here!! & this ballpoint And here my Prison diary will be on the tabel wating fr you when you come & Ill be gone.

So now I got to say goodby My Freind. & I got to say SORRY. Please tell Eric & Sam I say SORRY an I love them & Im sorry abt everything I did & killing ther mom & try to forgive me & then forget me. & if you can help them My Freind. & I say SORY to you My Freind. Rember you said last time I saw you when I was still inside last time you visited me an you said you was a bad frend to me you try to help & you give me things but it all hurts me & it hurts you & don't do any good for anybody & you said you nevr shd be my frend it was wrong an it brok the rules for being volunteer so it ws wrong and you said "Im just yr Enabler know what an Enabler is Thats wht I hav becom" you said that & you cried Im just yr enabler. But I say you are My Freind & I am yr Freind & I love you. And you tried to do good for me & you did.

The WATCH is fr you so you can keep bettr time & make more money MisterAbbot!!? My mom gave it to me for my birthday. An the RING is for Eric. You gave it to me rember??!

Now I got to get ready to go. Then Ill put out the light & then put out the light.

From YR FREIND Derek

ELEVEN
Snow and Dandelions

Oh - hullo there. I'm so glad you woke me, my dear. Oh no, you mustn't apologize. I spend so much time sleeping - much too much time sleeping. I'd rather not, but there's so little to do here - I just lie and meditate and think back over my life. I would have been so sad if you'd come and gone without rousing me so we can talk. Our final talk, perhaps. I *have* enjoyed our talks, my dear. Although *I* do most of the talking, don't I? You're such a patient listener!

No - of course don't turn it off! I promised you, didn't I, you could record whatever and whenever you like, for your Gerontology project - "Life-stories of hospitalized seniors", was that its title? I haven't been much good for you so far, though, I think! Just a silly old lady maundering on about this and that - but if you can find anything worthy of inclusion in your dissertation, I would be honoured! It's like a last will and testament. Only I've got so little to give you, just the fruits of a misspent life! Oh yes, it *has* been - you'll see; I'll tell you all about that this time!

Oh and look, it's sunny outside now. It was such a grey day when I fell asleep. And now the sunlight is so lovely on the snow, isn't it? Like milk, creamy milk. You brought the sun with you, my dear! Just as you bring sunshine into my life. And I do have a secret to tell you, but not just yet!

Did they tell you that I will be leaving soon? No, that's not the secret! They've found a place for me. No, they wouldn't tell you, would they? They keep Volunteers in ignorance for the good of their souls!

Confidentiality, that's what it's called! I forgot. I am just a forgetfu: old lady now. No, don't shake your head, my dear; I am, I know I am. It comes to us all. Old age - yes, and death. It'll come to you too - one day you'll be - Oh, I almost told you my secret! But yes, they've found a place for me - at last, at last - and they say it is a very good nursing-home, and I'll be very happy there. Well, we'll see.

But I'm babbling on, and I haven't even asked after *you*. I hope you had a truly joyful Christmas, my dear. A serene Christmas. And now it's back for the new term? I hope it will be a good one for you. I'm sure it will be. You must have been glad to spend that time with your parents and your sister, and did you see other relatives? And your friends, some of your friends? I'm so glad. Those things really matter, trust an old lady. *They really matter*. They're more important than almost anything else. But you know that - I know you do, a kind-hearted intelligent girl like you. I know you do, my dear. But it's easy to forget it, sometimes. You can make such terrible mistakes; you can forget how easily people can be hurt, especially those nearest and dearest, the very ones you don't want to hurt most of all. Even by what you *don't* do. *Especially* by what you don't do, sometimes. And sometimes the hurt can go on and on and on, and ruin whole lives. Always try to remember that. Remember what a silly old lady said when you visited her! And don't ever assume that wisdom comes with age. Some of us go on doing the same silly wicked things to the bitter end. You just run out of excuses - and eventually time! You have to work so hard for wisdom., and even then there's change and chance -

Yes, our last time together, perhaps. I know you would go on visiting me if you could, my dear, yes I know that, but you have lots of other things, more important things, to do. You have a busy life and your studying - and what about your boyfriend, doesn't he deserve some time with you, now? - don't neglect him! Besides I would be depriving other patients here of your cheerful company. I wouldn't want that! Did I tell you that I was once a hospital Volunteer myself, like you? Not in this hospital, one of the other ones in Hamilton - the General. And I always hated it when I'd come into the ward one day and find the bed empty, and the room being cleaned - and you didn't know whether the patient had been moved to another ward or to another hospital or to a nursing-home, or had died in the night. And noone told you. And then I'd be so sad and wish I could've said goodbye. And really it was silly - we've all got to die, haven't we? Sooner or later.

Oh I must try to talk sense. And I must try not to ramble and babble - I always despised people who did that! Yes, I despised people too easily. I know that now. It took me a long time to learn. Teachers are not good at learning, you know! They naturally think they know everything! But people are kinder than you think, and forgive. *You* have been so kind, my dear, visiting me. You have become my closest friend, do you know that? Yes - but you mustn't feel you should come any more than you have done - not even that much now, my dear - you have your own life and responsibilities, and they must come first. I was a Volunteer like you, oh years ago - before I fell ill, before I became such a feeble sick old lady. It's hard to be dependent, trust me - you have to learn how to do it. And trust me, it's hard, it's hard. Especially if you've been so active, if you've valued your independence as much as I did. Oh how I did! God taught me a really hard lesson when he took that away, and so suddenly. One day I was still teaching and volunteering, so active, and then I had a fall, just a silly fall, on a patch of ice, I was in too much of a hurry - and then, just when I thought I was back to normal, fully recovered, this silly stroke -

Did I tell you all this? Oh yes I'm sure I did and you're too polite to say so, my dear. I'm just a garrulous silly old lady now - garrulous silly *sick* old lady! Who'd have thought it. How does that poem go - "No memory of having starred Can keep the end from being hard." And I never even starred! Yes, Robert Frost. I've always loved his poems. I tried hard to persuade my students to like them too, and some did. Sometimes it all seems so long ago - so very long ago. I must have told you about my years as a teacher? Yes, I thought so. You know such a lot, my dear, you're interested in everything, poems as well as your Gerontology studies - that's the way to live a full life, to enjoy life and give enjoyment to others - I would have loved having you in my class!

No, I didn't have any visitors while you were away - not even another Volunteer. But I did have a telephone call from someone - someone who will be visiting me tomorrow, someone very special. And the nurses were so kind and pleasant, and we had singsongs and carols, and there was a Christmas dinner - a choir from one of the local churches came round too.

I'll tell you something now that I wouldn't have told you before, my dear. But this still isn't my secret! Did I mention to you that I have a son, a few years older than you? No, that's Jon, the one you met visiting me - he and Beth are my *step-children*, strictly speaking - they're a few years younger than my son. Yes, well, my son's in prison. He's been in prison, in and out, for about eight years. Since he was younger than you; that's when he first got into trouble with the law, for breaking into a store to steal liquor and attacking a man in there who tried to stop him. You see, my son is ill. He is a chronic alcoholic. He gets angry and violent when he wants alcohol. It's an illness, and nobody has been able to cure him yet. He's been in AA groups and had treatment, and they prescribe pills and - I won't tell you all the details, my dear. Just trust me, alcoholism is the curse of the devil. Addiction to drugs is too - but I know through my son what suffering is caused by addiction to alcohol - for him, for those who love him, for so many people, so many many many. I lie here and think about them all, and then it's as if the silence is groaning. Sometimes I wake up and think I must have been screaming or moaning in my sleep, like that man in the next room who used to wake us up in the night with all his crying and yelling - the nurses said it was memories of the War, things he couldn't forget, poor man, poor man. And they said he was shouting, in Polish I think it was, "Kill, kill, kill them all!" You just long to do something to cure it, to end the suffering, and you can't, and that's the worst form of suffering, perhaps - seeing what it's doing to him, to your own son, that it's *killing* him and everyone around him, kill, kill, kill, kill, and not being able to do anything about it. And knowing that you are responsible for it, too.

No, my dear, I *am*. I know that. Trust me, I know that. You can argue about the extent of responsibility, you know, but not about the responsibility itself. I am responsible. I *am* responsible. And soon I'll be facing my Maker - I dread that - unless He doesn't want me and Satan claims me and I go down to Hell, to the eternal flames of Hell. That is what I deserve. But God is merciful too. Do you mind my talking like this to you, my dear? You must say if it is upsetting you and I'll stop. I don't want *you* to suffer too! But you may learn from my sins. And it is so good to tell someone. A priest came just before Christmas. He was an Anglican, as I am. Vicar of a church in Westdale. You know I am from England, don't you? I still have an English accent, slightly, people tell me. I came to Canada - to Hamilton - in 1961, when I was twenty-six. Two of my uncles had immigrated here after the War. One came to Hamilton to work at Stelco - he was an engineer, he'd worked in a munitions factory in the War - and I lived with him and my aunt at first. *He* was English too, I think - the priest. Such a kind man, he had a lovely face. He told me about his disabled daughter, how he loved her, how hard it was for his wife to look after her day after day. But I couldn't talk to him. He asked if I wanted to confess, and I couldn't. I knew I should, but I couldn't. It is so long since I went into a church. I just couldn't. But I can talk to you, my dear. But perhaps I shouldn't? That's one of the values of Volunteers, isn't it? I was a Volunteer, you know - before I fell ill. Patients would tell me things that they couldn't tell anyone else - family, friends, doctor, nurses, anyone. They knew I wouldn't tell anyone else because I was a Volunteer. They knew that what they told me would stay with me - it was confidential - and anyway I didn't know any of the people, as you don't know my son and never will.

So let me tell you. It's a sort of confession! Isn't that strange - here I am, confessing to you, not the priest! But you don't need to forgive me. I don't think anyone can forgive me. I can't forgive myself. Perhaps even God won't be able to forgive me. If you can just listen, my dear.

I fell in love. In England, I mean - I was a young teacher, just out of training-college; but the man was looking after his widowed mother and said he could never marry me. It was in the years after the War. That's when I decided to emigrate to Canada. I applied for a teaching post here and taught English and History in a high-school for over ten years. Then I fell pregnant with my son. As I say, wisdom doesn't necessarily come with years. I was lonely and he - the father of my son - was a very attractive man: handsome, intelligent, ambitious, generous - and married. I even knew Caroline, his wife. They were next-door neighbours of my uncle and aunt, who had invited me to dinner to meet them - I had my own little apartment by then. He was a few years younger than me, a successful businessman, and also a School Trustee at that time - it was the beginning of his political career. I won't tell you his name, but it's well-known in Hamilton - and beyond. And I won't bore you with details about how our affair began and how it progressed. He would come to my apartment, in the late afternoon. There was honesty between us - to a point, anyway; there can't be *complete* honesty in an affair, which is intrinsically deceitful, isn't it? I was so grateful to him for his love. I knew I would do anything for him. But -

Yes, it ended. It ended because, to my astonishment, I fell pregnant - this was 1972, I was nearly forty, and we had been so careful. I don't blame him. I never did. And I knew that I must either have an abortion - but I didn't know how to go about that, there were no clinics in those days - or any that I knew about, and I couldn't ask anyone. Either I must have an abortion, or I must go away, and have the baby. And I did - I couldn't bear the thought of an abortion, anyway. But it was so hard to leave him. He was so hurt, hurt more than angry, I think - he couldn't understand why I was suddenly saying that it was over and I was going away. And of course he never knew - could never have guessed - that I did it for him partly, to save him from what would have happened if anyone ever knew about our affair. His marriage would have ended, I'm sure - Caroline would have left him and taken the two children. And his political career would have been destroyed just as it was beginning to prosper.

So I went. I told him I no longer loved him, and I gave up my teaching - fortunately it was close to summer when I discovered I was pregnant - and I went to Kingston, where my other uncle was, and his wife helped me - She was a truly kind and loving woman, Aunt Dora, she even looked after my son in his earlier years, when I had to go out to work. But I knew it wouldn't be easy and it wasn't. Being a single mother in those days was an extreme social stigma, my dear - very different from today. And the birth itself was a hard one, because I wasn't young. I was very lucky to have Aunt Dora - she even kept it from my parents in England; they never knew, they would have been so upset. The five years I lived with her and Uncle Ken, the first five years of Derek's life - that was such a happy time, the happiest time in my life - until they decided to move out West, to Vancouver. They died years ago - I lost touch with them, another of my sins - and they never had any children of their own. So - But I had my baby. A beautiful baby boy, and I called him Derek. Not a family name, I just happened to like it. And I wasn't ashamed, really, about having an illegitimate baby - a baby out of wedlock, as they used to say then. No, I was not ashamed. Children don't need birth certificates to make them precious. But I *am* ashamed of what I did after that. I am even ashamed to tell you. But you will learn from it, my dear, I think, and be an even better person than you are. I hope you aren't bored or disgusted with what I'm telling you? Sure?

One thing troubles me still. Should I have told Derek who his father was? I never did. Do you think I should have? But I thought it would just cause pain to everyone. To Derek's father, who was now wealthy and prominent, an MP too, in the Ontario Government; to Caroline; and to their two daughters; even to Derek, especially if his father didn't want to acknowledge him. I saw Caroline a few times after I was back in Hamilton; I remember once in the supermarket, there she was suddenly, with her twin girls and I was struggling to keep Jon and Beth in order, and I just smiled at her, and she smiled back - perhaps she didn't remember quite who I was. And I saw Derek's father too, once or twice, but never close enough to have to talk to him, thank goodness. And he'd moved away from where my Uncle and Aunt lived, to Dundas and then to one of those mansions in Ancaster - he became very prosperous, and influential in the community. But perhaps I was wrong. I think I was. Perhaps he would have helped Derek. Perhaps he would have wanted to know he had a son, and be Derek's father. Of course he never knew he had a son - he still doesn't. Yes, perhaps I was wrong.

Perhaps I put my silly egotistical concerns above Derek's well-being. Yes, I did. I did. But that isn't what I am ashamed of. If I was wrong about that, I don't think that was truly a sin. I tried to do what was right. I was wrong, but I tried to do the right thing.

But what I did to Derek when he was a little boy *was* a sin. I got married, to a divorced man with a son and a daughter, and I abandoned Derek. No - I can see how shocked you are, my dear, and so you should be. It was a terrible sin. I didn't mean to. Of course I didn't mean to. At the time, I even told myself I *wasn't* doing that, I *wasn't* abandoning him. When Uncle Ken and Aunt Dora left, I already knew the man, he was from Hamilton, the son of one of Uncle Tom's friends - we had met in Hamilton and he was visiting Kingston, and even before they left he asked me to marry him. I didn't love him, but I liked him, and I was sorry for his children, and no doubt I liked the idea of being their mother, and being respectably married at last. Derek was five years old then, and the other two, Jon and Beth, were two and three years old. And I wanted to go back to Hamilton and be close to my Uncle and Aunt there - I knew that Derek's father wouldn't want to have any connection with me, after what had happened between us, even if we chanced to meet - and we never actually did. What I never expected was that Rod would dislike Derek. He had seemed to get on well with Derek before our marriage, but soon afterwards I realized that he didn't think of Derek in any way like he did of his own two children. But I didn't want to see that - I pretended I didn't see that for a long while. And it just got worse and worse, and I closed my eyes to it to keep the peace.

Well, I did keep the peace. My marriage survived for a while. But the price was paid by Derek. He was the sacrifice. Rod would beat him for the smallest thing and humiliate him in front of the other children and shut him outside in the cold, and he got more and more angry and violent - I could see it happening, like a nightmare that got darker and uglier every moment. Sometimes Derek would lose his temper and hit Jon and Beth and they would scream and he'd get beaten for that. And I did nothing to help him - if I defended him the slightest bit, Rod would explode in fury, and hurt him even more. I did try to comfort him and help him when I could, but it was hard, with the other children, and looking after Rod, too - he was very demanding, very critical of my housekeeping and how I was bringing up Jon and Beth - and I suppose I was frightened at the back of my mind that he might leave and I'd be on my own again. My mother had died by then, and my father had remarried - and anyway I didn't want to go back to England. And then

Derek's teachers complained that he was hitting and hurting the other children in his class, and swearing, refusing to obey, and then he was expelled for - oh I can't remember what it was for - there were so many things by then. He was hated and feared by all the neighbours, they all talked about him as a really bad boy, their kids were told to keep away from him. Rod kept on threatening to throw him out of the house, I had to beg and beg him not to - and anyway he spent most of his time out, on the street - I didn't know where he was most of the time, he wouldn't tell me. It was horrible. So unfair too. Of course he fell in with a gang of other neglected boys, and they would all spend their time on the street and who knows where, smoking and drinking and who knows what else - and then he got caught stealing wine in the LCBO - he was already drinking heavily, I think, on his way to alcoholism.

And in the end it didn't save my marriage anyway. Rod walked out on me after I found that he was having affairs with women in his company - someone wrote to me anonymously. Jon and Beth were teenagers then, and they were very resentful - they blamed me, though I could never understand why. Perhaps it was because I never told them about Rod's affairs - I didn't want them to turn against him. They didn't exactly turn against me either, I don't mean that, but Rod was rich - an executive in a big company - and after our separation I didn't have a lot of money - Rod gave me some, but I had to work again and I was fortunate that the School Board were prepared to have me back. They said I had an excellent record from my first period of teaching in Hamilton. Jon and Beth would live part of the time with me, and part with Rod, usually weekends when he had time to treat them, take them to meals and films - he never remarried, he died five years ago, of cancer, suddenly. The children are in their twenties now. Beth isn't married - she's studying Engineering at McMaster, she lives with her boyfriend. But Jon's married. No children - I think his wife doesn't want any - she's a doctor, and she wants her career - so many young women put that first now, don't they? They came twice to visit me, soon after the operation, and they phone sometimes. I think they still blame me deep down. Of course we can always blame people for any of our unhappiness and problems, can't we? We can always do that. If so, I deserve it. I do. Not for anything I did to Rod and the two of them, but for what I did to Derek.

Oh Derek! Derek, Derek! And now he's taken my grandchildren from me and that is the worst suffering of all for me. But I do deserve it. And I really like the woman he was living with - Nancy. We got on well together, she's not an educated girl and comes from a broken family and grew up in poverty, but she's a loving girl, and when I first fell ill, when I'd had that fall and was home in bed, some time before this silly stroke, she would come, with Eric - he was a still a baby then - and she would cook me a meal and help me with keeping the apartment clean, and we'd play games and have such a happy time together. Eric isn't really my grandchild, Derek isn't his father - only the girl, Samantha, is. But they are both such lovely lovely lovely children, and I think of them both as my grandchildren, and they *are* my grandchildren. She would let them be with me on their own, too, later, when they were a bit older, or I would babysit them in her apartment - and she would bring them for the day and they'd help me in my little garden - children love gardening, all children do, there's no greater joy than seeing things grow, blossoming in the sun. Oh I love those two children. Oh my dear, I love them. But now I won't ever see them again, because Derek attacked her - he was in a drunken rage - he hurt Eric too, when he tried to defend his mother. Nancy called the police - she had to - and they took Derek off in handcuffs and he was sentenced to two years I think it was - he's in prison now.

But I'll be seeing him tomorrow. Nancy telephoned to say she and he would come on the way to their apartment - it's nearby. He hasn't been in touch at all, recently - it's hard from prison, I know - so I'm looking forward to seeing him more than I can tell you, and hoping so much that everything will go well this time. He promised her he'd never drink again and I think this time he won't, he won't, because he's got so much to live for, a loving wife and children, a family, a home. Oh but I miss my grandchildren, so much, so much. I think I would do anything, *anything*, to see them again, but Nancy would hardly talk to me before she telephoned last week - I think I understand why, and she can't blame me more than I blame myself - and I was terrified that she would go away with the children, far away - and sometimes she would just put the phone down when I called her and she heard my voice, so then I stopped phoning. I tried to talk to her several times, before I had this last stroke and found myself back again in hospital. And I wrote to her, and I sent birthday cards and presents to Eric and Samantha, but I don't know if Nancy even let them have what I sent - I haven't heard from them at all, not a thank-you note or a telephone call - nothing, nothing, nothing. From day to day, just nothing. But perhaps it will be different from tomorrow. She just phoned out of the blue a week or so ago to say Derek was coming out tomorrow and they would come straight here to see me on their way home. She knows how badly I want to see him - see them all. I'm so excited about it - perhaps that's

why I've wanted so much to talk about it all - I am so longing to see
Derek and Nancy and the two children - my grandchildren, my Eric
and Samantha.

No, that's not my secret either! Though it could have been and it
is connected! I *will* tell you, I'm not just teasing you - but first, my
dear, I want to say how grateful I am to you for listening all this time.
I hope it hasn't upset you at all, any of it. Anyway, I've finished. I've
told you my life story, haven't I? The life story of a boring forgetful sick
dependent silly *wicked* old lady. Old, old. "The inescapable lousiness
of growing old." Have you heard that before? Yes - you *are* well-read,
my dear! Irving Layton. He's one of the best Canadian poets, isn't he?
So full of passion. It was about his mother, when she was dying. I always thought it was a marvellous poem, so full of love - anguish and
love. Well, there's always anguish in love. And I always loved that other
poem of his, about the little calf - yes, I can see you know it. And now
he's old too. Alzheimer's? I didn't know that. In the *Globe and Mail*?
Just the other day. But why would they put that in the paper? So cruel.
And for those who love him. Don't you think so? What a terrible fate
for a man who has always loved words, made joy out of words. Here
am I grousing about being in bed when he has lost the words that were
his life and happiness! I'm so sorry. I almost wish you hadn't told me.
No, I don't mean that, my dear, but it *is* very sad to hear about.

But you know, I do think he was wrong - "inescapable lousiness of
growing old". No, I think old age can be beautiful, noble, wise, serene.
I've seen that and you must have too. Even in hospital - I was a Volunteer too, like you. But it's a matter of luck, to some extent - and genes
and other things you can't control. Still, we do have something to say
about it, I think - most of the time anyway. We can be cheerful, we can
control ourselves when we're in pain so as not to upset other people,
especially those we love. You must have learnt all about it in your Gerontology classes? No, not "inescapable lousiness". But the person who
said you have to be tough to grow old, he was right - or she. And most
of all, you must be grateful for the privilege of old age, to still be here
after so many years, still able to enjoy God's beautiful earth, and the
love and kindness of people like you, my dear. So many die young.

I was in London during the Battle of Britain, the air-raids, when I
was a child - but I told you that, didn't I? In the West End. Well, it's a
long story, I'll tell you all about it next time if you're interested. And a
bomb fell on a house along the street - quite near. I remember the noise,
the explosion, even now, and the screaming and crying - so many died.
One of them was a little boy I used to play with, his mother and my

mother were friends, and the mother was killed too, and I remember just squatting under the stairs and weeping, weeping, and asking God "Why did he die, why not me, why am I still alive?" And - Strange - I've just remembered that his name was Derek too. Yes, it *was* - Derek. Perhaps - Well, soon after that, as the bombing got worse, sirens all the time, explosions, and I remember those nights in the crowded Underground shelters and, if you couldn't get there in time, the nights spent cowering all together under the stairs - I was so frightened, but we were also so close to each other - but then we children were sent into the countryside, evacuated, "Vackies" they called us, and I had to look after my two brothers because I was the eldest - and that separated us from our parents, and then we three were separated too, and it was never possible for us to be a family again after the War, somehow. My parents tried, they were good kind people, they loved us and we loved them, but the War - How different it would have been, I sometimes think - though it's futile to speculate, isn't it? - if there'd never been a War. But there *was* a War and it changed everything. Like the first one, the Great War. Not just for us, my family, my generation, but also future generations. That's a real horror of war, my dear - The death and suffering at the time, buildings burning, the bombs, the explosions - all that is horrible, horrible. But it's the way it goes on into the future, on and on, destroying happiness. Pray God, my dear, never another war.

But those are the memories I don't welcome! I used to have nightmares, too, for many years. Now I hardly ever even dream, and when I do my dreams aren't always unhappy, thank goodness. Last night I dreamt about Derek - not about the past, or even the present, but I think the future. He was handsome and happy, smiling, at ease with himself and the whole world, and he was walking towards me, and the most beautiful sunset was glowing behind him. Then he stopped and held out his arms to me. And I just said "Derek, Derek." And we embraced, there in the sunshine.

And poetry gives me joy too. The poems I taught in class and the ones I didn't! As I lie here, I remember little scraps and I repeat them over and over, loving every word, every sound, the rhythm, the music. Do you ever do that? They are very good company, poems. I recommend them highly! Believe an old sick lady. Another scrap came into my mind just now, while I was talking about Irving Layton's poem about his mother dying. This one comes from very long ago in my life, when I was in my English girls' school, just after the War, years before I came to Canada, and we had a wonderful English mistress, who inspired me so much. I even imitated the way she spoke, and I wanted so badly to become a teacher like her. She was so passionate about a poet called Thomas - Edward Thomas. He died in the First World War. I think she was related to the woman who loved him - she was a poet too. I loved one of the poems she read to us - she had a lovely warm voice - I can hear it even now. The poet was walking in the English countryside at nightfall - how I used to love walking in the countryside, too, in the hills around the school, just after the War! And he heard an owl calling. How did that poem go? How we should be so grateful for what we have, all the joys and comforts of life - In an inn, that's right, he comes inside from the dark and cold, and he finds "food, fire, and rest", the necessities and comforts of life. And then he hears the owl's cry - "a most melancholy cry shaken out long and clear upon the hill" - and that reminds him of how so many people don't have any of the things he has, they don't even have any protection, "all who lie under the stars, Soldiers and poor, unable to rejoice." Yes. And you know, I heard an owl last night. I know I did. In my dream, it must have been, in my dream about Derek. No, it couldn't have been - owls don't hoot during the day, do they? It must have been before, or after. But I can't quite place it. Perhaps it was after. But I know I did hear it.

So many things one can't be sure about. So many things one doesn't know - can't know. But that doesn't matter in the end, one mustn't be disheartened - that's what life is like. Mystery. The heart of life is mystery! Never be frightened of mystery, my dear. If you're frightened of that, you're frightened of life itself, the heart of life. Trust your instinct, trust the beating of your own heart. Trust love. Or am I talking nonsense again?

Well, my dear, enough from this garrulous old lady! More than enough! How patient you have been to listen to me rambling on about my life and times. I do appreciate it. How can I ever repay the gift you have given me in your visits, and listening to me? I can only offer a silly old lady's thoughts about life. I hope you won't laugh, I don't have any great insights. But I think the strong should always protect the weak, and the rich and fortunate should always give to the poor and unlucky. And that applies to all of us, doesn't it, because there is always someone weaker or poorer or more unfortunate than us, needing our support. Life always seems so complicated, it gets more and more complicated, doesn't it? But I think what we have to do to help others, which is the same as helping ourselves, is to care about them - especially children, we must all protect and care about children; the old may need help from the middle-aged, when we get weak or sick, but we must all help children; they will become us, and only if we love them can they learn how to love *their* children. So it does all come back to love, my dear. As simple as that: love, love, love. And you know that anyway: we all know that, somewhere deep down, unless we have been too deeply hurt, unless we have allowed our hearts to harden. That's what this silly old lady says!

No, no, Nurse, I'm fine. Please don't be concerned about me - I have been having the most wonderful conversation, perhaps the best in all my life, with this very dear, very patient friend - I don't feel at all tired and weak, I feel invigorated, thanks to her! But I know it's suppertime - and our conversation is almost over. Just a few more minutes? Thank you.

Oh no, no, I hadn't forgotten. My little secret, my little secret! There is a clue, you know, on the table beside my bed. Those two cards. From Jon and Beth. Yes, read them, my dear. Yes, my birthday! Tomorrow. Do you know, I'll be seventy! Who would have predicted it - to live that long! I'm so looking forward to tomorrow! Thank you, my dear. No, of course you must do no such thing. That would make me feel embarrassed to have told you! Your presence here today is my birthday present, and a very precious present it has been, and is. Believe an old lady! Thank you, thank you. Will you kiss me? On my cheek? Yes. Thank you. And pray for me if you think of it.

It'll soon be quite dark out there, my dear. Time for you to go! Back to your own life. Mine's almost over, and yours is just beginning. Winter and spring! I wonder if there'll be any snow tonight? We've had so much this winter already, haven't we? And I hear the nurses complaining about it. "Too much, too much already" they say. Yes, the roads and sidewalks must be causing some problems, I know, and accidents. But I love the snow. I've always loved the snow. People think of it as negative, but for me it is so positive. Pure and positive. I told you about how I used to love gardening, didn't I? Yes, well, it was the snow that would preserve my roses from the icy cold every winter - from extinction, from death - so they could revive in spring, and fill the air with the sweet scent of their lovely blossoms in summer. Lovely lovely lovely blossoms. So many blossoms, God has filled our world with blossoms - and do you know - oh, this is a shocking confession, my dear - you mustn't tell a soul! My favourite flower of all isn't the rose, doesn't even have a scent, and it's as common as dirt, and people think of it as ugly, a weed, to be exterminated at any cost - but it's as bright and cheerful and vigorous as the sun, whole fields of it, fields and fields of it, and on all the lawns, every spring, and it'll never never never be defeated. Can you guess? The dandelion! I love the dandelion! Under the snow its seeds are waiting. And soon the snow will get dirty, and melt into slush and be so very troublesome and ugly and even dangerous. But only so spring can come!

Goodbye, my dear. Fare well. God be with you.